NEVER to be TOLD

BECKY CITRA

ORCA BOOK PUBLISHERS

for Janet

BC

Text copyright © 2006 Becky Citra

Library and Archives Canada Cataloguing in Publication

Citra, Becky
Never to be told / Becky Citra.

ISBN 10: 1-55143-567-5 / ISBN 13: 978-1-55143-567-1

I. Title.

PS8555.I87N49 2006   jC813'.54   C2006-902720-X

First published in the United States, 2006
Library of Congress Control Number: 2006927095

Summary: Twelve-year-old Asia's world is turned upside down by family secrets and ghostly encounters.

Orca Book Publishers gratefully acknowledges the support for its publishing programs provided by the following agencies: the Government of Canada through the Book Publishing Industry Development Program and the Canada Council for the Arts, and the Province of British Columbia through the BC Arts Council and the Book Publishing Tax Credit.

Design and typesetting: Christine Toller
Cover artwork & cover design: Cathy Maclean

ORCA BOOK PUBLISHERS
PO BOX 5626, STATION B
VICTORIA, BC CANADA
V8R 6S4

ORCA BOOK PUBLISHERS
PO BOX 468
CUSTER, WA USA
98240-0468

www.orcabook.com
Printed and bound in Canada.
Printed on 100% PCW recycled paper.
010 09 08 07 • 6 5 4 3 2

One crow for sorrow
Two for joy
Three for a girl
Four for a boy
Five for silver
Six for gold
Seven for a secret
Never to be told.

English counting rhyme

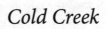

Cold Creek

...from the diary of Miranda Williams

May 18, 1915

Today a stranger came to Cold Creek. He rode out of the mountains, mounted on a big black stallion and leading a packhorse. Our farm is remote but we have had visitors before. I don't know why I feel this sense of foreboding.

His name is Ridley Blackmore, and he is looking for work. Since George is away until tomorrow buying cattle, I instructed the man to pitch his tent by the creek, where there is plenty of dry wood for a fire, and wait there.

As he turned to go, a movement on the back of his packhorse caught my eye. For one foolish second I thought I saw Daisy's face peering from a bundle of furs. My legs turned to jelly, and I am sure my heart stopped beating.

A little girl wiggled out of the furs, and I saw then that she is not at all like Daisy. Her face is thinner and her hair is straight and dull. Blackmore introduced her, rather indifferently, as his daughter Beatrice.

I know I was staring. Beatrice looked about three, the same age our Daisy was when the Lord took her away. I said hello to her, but Blackmore informed me abruptly that she doesn't speak. Doesn't speak! When I think how well Daisy spoke at that age!

I am sitting by the window as I write this. I can see Blackmore's shadow moving between his tent and the fire. I can't see Beatrice, but of course she must be fast asleep by now. I will never tell George that I mistook the stranger's little girl for Daisy. He would look at me with that mixture of alarm and pity that I hate so much. He would say it is one more reason that I must consult a doctor.

Montgomery has just come home, and he is meowing for his supper. I am exhausted, but I know I will not sleep tonight.

CHAPTER ONE

Asia found the moth on the kitchen windowsill behind a pot of parsley. Its fragile wings, the color of milk, were tinged pale gray at the tips. She cupped it in her hand and gently touched its furry body.

"It's so beautiful!" she breathed, carrying it carefully to the pine table where Maddy was kneading bread.

Maddy stared at the moth. Her face turned as pale as the moth's wings. She said quietly, "Put your other hand over it. Don't let it get away."

Asia covered the moth. It fluttered in the warm pocket of her hands. Something in Maddy's voice frightened her. Maddy saw signs in everything. She had taught Asia to keep her eyes peeled for four-leaf clovers, to slice the bread from one end only and to tuck a lucky penny in her shoe at night.

"What's wrong?" said Asia.

"I just don't like it, that's all." Maddy opened the screen door and pushed Asia out with a floury hand. "Make sure you take it far away from the house before you let it go." She closed the door firmly behind her.

Asia blinked in the bright sunshine. From the porch she gazed across the banks of Cold Creek, over the sloping meadows and pine-covered hills, all the way to the slate-gray peaks of the distant mountains. It was going to be another blazing hot day. Already the sky was a dark hard blue. Maddy's sheep huddled in the shade of the trees beside the house, and the chickens had disappeared inside their shed.

On the other side of the creek, a man in faded brown coveralls and a wide-brimmed hat trudged across the meadow toward the log bridge. It was Ira, and he was carrying something in his arms. Something big and bulky. Asia frowned, trying to make out what it was.

The moth bumped against her fingers. She stepped off the porch and walked through the grass, holding her hands close to her chest. When she thought she was far enough from the house, she opened her fingers and the moth fluttered away like a ghost. She glanced back and saw Maddy at the window, watching her. Then she ran across the bridge to meet Ira.

His arms were full of yellow and brown fur. It was Dandy, the old dog who had been part of Cold Creek since before Asia came to live with Maddy and Ira. Dandy's milky eyes stared dully at Asia.

"I found him over at the gopher hill," said Ira. He carried Dandy the rest of the way to the house. Her heart pounding with fear, Asia ran ahead. "Maddy!" she yelled. "Maddy! Come quickly!"

Maddy came outside, wiping her hands on her apron, the screen door banging behind her. She glanced at Ira's face and then rested her hand on Dandy's still body. The dog gave a sudden shudder and slumped even deeper into Ira's arms.

"He's gone," said Maddy. She looked terribly sad, but not shocked. She stroked Dandy's yellow ear, the one with the tear in it. "Good old fellow," she murmured. "Good dog."

Tears flooded Asia's cheeks. Maddy drew her close, pressing Asia's face into her apron. "Oh, my girl."

Asia breathed in Maddy's warm bread scent. "You knew," she whispered. "How?"

"It was the moth." Maddy held Asia tighter. "A white moth in a house is a messenger of death."

～

"Dandy was old. He would've died, moth or no moth," said Ira. "He was...let's see, ninety-eight in people years."

He and Asia were in the workshop, a log building with big windows that faced the creek. Ira was making a cross for Dandy's grave.

He glanced sideways at Asia, who sat on a stool beside him, sifting sawdust between her fingers. "Sometimes our Maddy gets carried away with her superstitions."

He smoothed the rough edges of the pine boards with a scrap of sandpaper. "You have to set your mind on all the good times in Dandy's long life. Hunting gophers in the meadow, chewing stew bones, sleeping in his basket by the woodstove."

"Going for walks along the creek. Chasing Maddy's chickens, " Asia added.

She felt drained. With a sigh she pushed the sawdust into a tidy pile and slid off the stool. She wandered around the workshop, looking at Ira's handcrafted boxes.

The boxes, lined up on long shelves, were ready to be wrapped and mailed to customers, or taken to Cariboo Curios, the gift shop in town. They were all different sizes and had smooth polished sides and lids inlaid with delicate pieces of dark and light wood in the shapes of birds and animals.

What Asia loved best about the boxes were the secret compartments. Every box had one, tucked under a false bottom or behind a drawer or even in a lid. Asia knew all of Ira's tricks. For as long as she could remember, she had watched him work. When she was little, while Ira measured and sawed and planed, she had sat on the floor and gathered handfuls of pale wood shavings and dropped them like snowflakes on her hair. Now that she was twelve, she helped Ira, sanding the boxes until they were satiny smooth and polishing the gleaming wood with a soft rag.

Ira finally put down his tools and held up the finished cross for her approval. "You take this back to the house and put some words on it. Something fitting for a fine dog. And then we'll get Maddy and say a proper goodbye to Dandy."

"The gopher hill was Dandy's stomping ground," said Maddy. "It's only right to bury him in the place he loved best."

So Ira carried him back across the bridge and through the meadow, this time wrapped in the old wool blanket from his basket. Maddy brought a shovel and Asia carried the cross. She trailed behind, setting the cross down in the long grass from time to time to pick wild daisies and purple fireweed for a funeral bouquet.

The ground at the gopher hill was hard. Ira was sweating and rubbing his brow by the time he'd dug the hole. He laid Dandy's body at the bottom and filled the hole in with dirt. Then he dug a smaller hole for the cross, on which Asia had carefully printed *Dandy, August 14, 2005. He will be deeply missed.*

Asia placed the flowers beside the cross. For a second, she had an odd prickly feeling that someone other than Maddy was standing beside her. A faint sound brushed her ear, and she heard a voice whisper *death*. She glanced around, astonished. A gentle breeze had picked up, rippling the long grass in the meadow. She frowned. There was no one else there except Ira and Maddy, and the only sound was the rustling of the aspen leaves by the creek.

They piled rocks on the grave to keep the coyotes from digging it up. Asia scrambled down the bank to the creek bed for one last look around. She couldn't escape that peculiar feeling that someone had been standing beside the grave, someone who had said the word death.

"Come on, Asia," called Maddy a few minutes later. "We're going back now."

Asia tossed a flat stone in the water and then climbed up the bank. On the way home, Ira had to stop for a few minutes, his hands resting on his knees as he took in big breaths.

"It's nothing," he protested when Maddy hovered. "Quit your fussing, woman. I'm just a bit played out from all that digging."

Asia gazed back across the meadow, her long black hair blowing away from her face. The tall grass shimmered in the heat. Dandy's cross stood pale and new against the dark blue sky.

CHAPTER TWO

Cold with shock, Miranda slipped into the grove of aspen trees. She hadn't meant to startle the girl. She hadn't meant to speak. The words had slipped out at the dog's grave. *Too much death.* And the girl had heard her. Miranda Williams had been dead for forty years, and this was the first time since her death that anyone had heard her speak.

She had been away from Cold Creek for a long time. Something had brought her back. Maybe it was the death of the old dog; she wasn't sure. She stared at the girl standing beside the grave. The woman had called her Asia. She had seen her from a distance on her other visits to Cold Creek, playing by the water or walking in the meadow, her long black hair blowing every which way in the breeze, but never before had she been this close to her.

A cat sprang out of the long grass and landed lightly on Miranda's shoulder. "There you are, Montgomery." She stroked his sleek gray back. His tail lashed from side to side. "You feel it too," she whispered. Her excitement grew, swelling inside her. *Too much death.* Her words hung over the dog's grave. And Asia had *heard.* After forty years, Miranda had made contact with a living person.

She was distressed at the changes in the man called Ira and the woman called Maddy. Ira's hair was now as white as snow, his face marked with deep lines. And Maddy grimaced when she stooped to pat the old dog one last time. Miranda knew all about growing old. She took one last look at Asia, who was trailing across the meadow behind the old people, and then turned the other way and walked over the hill toward the Old Farm.

The Old Farm was about half a mile from Maddy and Ira's house, at the bottom of a hill beside the creek. Miranda had come there as a young bride almost a hundred years ago, before the Great War. She paused at the top of the hill and gazed down at her old home. The roof on the log barn had collapsed, and a few scattered fence rails poked through the long grass. The two-story frame house was surrounded by weeds and nettles, and the porch sagged into the ground. "No," she whispered angrily. "Not again."

It was like this every time she came back, but it was always a shock. Her beloved home in ruins. Every time, it was harder to summon the strength to reverse the destruction. Her face contorted with effort as she shut out the image of the ruined farm and visualized instead lace curtains at the windows and flowers blooming around the porch. The back of her neck and spine tingled. The picture in front of her wavered and blurred like a reflection in a pond. After a few minutes, the tumbled-down buildings disappeared, and in their place nestled a snug, well-kept farm. Her breathing slowed. Everything was right again, and it would stay that way until she left.

Miranda drew in a breath and started down the hill. As she approached the house, her eyes were drawn reluctantly to the small square window tucked under the peak of the roof, the window in Daisy's little pink bedroom. Her chest tightened and she felt the familiar urgent need to go to her little girl. She closed her eyes and shuddered. Daisy was dead. She had been dead for over ninety years. Shivering, Miranda pulled her shawl around her shoulders. She had one more grave to visit, and then she would go inside her old house to rest. Even on this hot summer day, she was cold.

CHAPTER THREE

Maddy always said it didn't pay to ignore signs. A white moth in a house means business. It was foolish to let Ira take the tractor to the home meadow on a day so hot you could fry eggs on a rock, especially when anyone could see he wasn't feeling well. Losing Dandy had distracted her from the real danger.

"And of course," she would say later, "you can't tell a stubborn man like Ira anything. He wanted to finish the haying before the weather broke." When there were cattle at Cold Creek, Ira had hayed the upper meadow as well, working right through the long hot days of August and early September, until the hay shed was filled with sweet-smelling bales. Now there was only Maddy's handful of sheep to feed in the winter, and Ira could cut and bale enough hay in the home meadow in a few days.

Maddy rested in the shade on the porch, and Asia moved into the hammock under the trees with her new book. Asia could lose herself for hours in a good book, but this time her mind kept jumping back to Dandy. She had only read a few pages when Maddy squinted at the sky and then disappeared inside the house. She came back with a thermos of cold tea for Ira. "Go see what's keeping the old rascal," she said, with a hint of worry in her voice.

Asia got her bicycle out of the garage and strapped the thermos onto the back carrier. The road to the home meadow was just two ruts in the grass. She bumped along, missing Dandy's company. The sun burned through her T-shirt, and her long black hair felt like a heavy blanket on the back of her neck. She stopped once and sneaked a sip from the thermos. She rounded the last bend through the trees and paused at the edge of the meadow. Long rows of pale green cut grass shimmered in the sun.

Ira and the tractor were halfway down one row. Ira was slumped over the wheel, his hat fallen somewhere in the hay. The only sound was the click of a dragonfly's wings and the distant *tap tap tap* of a sapsucker.

Asia jumped off her bike, letting it topple to the ground, and ran to Ira.

CHAPTER FOUR

Asia stood beside the tractor and watched Maddy hurry across the field toward them. Maddy could sense trouble, and she must have waited just a few minutes before something told her to follow Asia.

Maddy took one look at Ira. Her face went white, but she said calmly, "Go back to the house and phone the Hildebrands. And then get the van."

Her voice faltered a tiny bit. "Hurry."

~

Asia gripped the steering wheel, bouncing on the hard seat as the van bumped across the field. Ira's tractor looked like an orange island in the middle of a pale green sea. She beeped the horn to tell Maddy she was coming and jammed the gas pedal down hard, ignoring the protesting whine of the tired engine. The van broke down all the time. Please, *please* don't choose today, she prayed.

Asia jerked the van to a stop beside the tractor. She jumped out. Ira had straightened up and was leaning against the back of the seat. His gray face glistened with a damp sheen of sweat.

"Get that old blanket out of the back," said Maddy. " Ira can lie down on it and we'll lift him in."

Ira had been staring at nothing, his breathing coming in ragged gasps. But he stirred at that. "Now, Mother," he said in a surprisingly clear voice, "I can walk to the van. Just give me a minute."

Ira sometimes called Maddy Mother, even though Harry, their only child, had grown up and left home twenty-five years ago. Goose bumps popped out along Asia's bare arms when Ira spoke. He was going to be okay.

She made a bed in the back of the van out of the old blanket and some empty feed sacks. Then she held onto one of Ira's arms and Maddy took the other and, step by slow step, they eased him off the tractor and into the van.

At the last minute, Ira said he couldn't go to town without his hat. Maddy said it was typical of Ira to turn stubborn in the middle of a crisis, but Asia spotted the hat on a mound of mowed grass and grabbed it.

It was a lucky thing that Ira had taught Asia to drive when she turned ten. He had tried to teach Maddy when they were first married. She had moved the car exactly two feet, let the clutch out too quickly and gasped when the car lurched to a stop. She sat there for a minute and then got out of the car and went into the house. That was the total of Maddy's driving experience.

Asia loved driving. By the time she turned twelve, she had driven the van, the tractor and the pickup truck all over Cold Creek, helping Ira haul water and bring in hay and firewood.

Asia glanced over her shoulder as the van bumped back across the field and up the grassy track to the road. Ira lay with his eyes closed, and Maddy was stretched out beside him, holding his hand.

When they turned onto the logging road to town, Maddy sat up and crawled into the front seat. "Keep over to the side more...there's a big pothole coming up around that corner...Lord, I hope we don't meet anyone."

Asia ignored her. If it weren't for Ira scaring her so badly, she would be enjoying this. Driving on the logging road was no different than driving through the fields. Easier actually. There were fewer ruts.

"Slow down a little," said Maddy.

"I phoned the Hildebrands," said Asia, to get Maddy's mind off her driving. Gert and Hans Hildebrand were their nearest neighbors, and they had known Maddy and Ira for years. "They're out, but Anna will tell them as soon as they get back."

"Good," said Maddy.

Anna and her younger sister Katya would be wildly jealous when they heard that she had driven the van to the hospital. Anna and Katya were the Hildebrand's granddaughters, and Katya was Asia's best friend. Anna and Katya spent the summers on their grandparents' ranch but they lived the rest of the year in Calgary where Katya said *nobody* Asia's age knew how to drive.

Suddenly Ira opened his eyes and said, "I don't like to complain, but I'm cooking back here."

To Asia's relief, Maddy disappeared into the back again. The side window creaked open, and Maddy settled herself against the side of the van. "I don't know why you keep doing this to me," she said.

"Now what's that supposed to mean?" said Ira weakly.

"We've been through this before. I blame it on your stubbornness. It was the same thing the day Asia came to live with us."

"Now Mother, that was nine years ago," protested Ira.

Asia could tell that Maddy was warming up. "Yes, and I distinctly remember telling you not to use the chainsaw that day. I told you I saw an owl sitting on the fence plain as day in the bright sun. You can't ask for a clearer sign of trouble. And sure enough, the next thing I knew, you were flat on your back by the woodpile."

Ira chuckled. "The blood was everywhere."

"How would you know?" said Maddy. "You were out cold."

Asia grinned. This was one of her favorite stories.

"I ran outside and said, 'Ira, you old fool, now what am I going to do?' Then I heard Asia and Sherri coming down the road."

"To be accurate," intervened Ira, "at the time, you didn't know Asia and her mom from a bean in the bush."

Maddy looked at Ira coldly. "Who's telling this story? I knew help was coming, didn't I? Sherri's truck had no muffler and it was making all kinds of racket. I ran up to the gate, waving my arms and hollering at her to stop."

Ira jumped in again. "I opened one eye and saw this tiny girl with pink cheeks and black hair shining down at me. I knew an angel had come to save me."

"Huh," said Maddy. "Asia is our angel, but you didn't know it then. You were in no state to be looking at angels. You were bleeding to death."

Asia suddenly thought of something. "Why were my mother and I just driving around that day? Were we supposed to be going somewhere else?"

There was a moment of silence in the back of the van before Maddy said, "There was a commune up past Cold Creek on the old King ranch. At the height of it, there were about six families living there. Sherri was trying to find it. Only problem was, the commune was gone. It just kind of fizzled out."

"Oh," said Asia. She tried to imagine living with all those families. She couldn't.

"But I know one thing," said Maddy. "It was meant to be. Your mother slid Ira into the back of her truck like he was a stick of firewood, and we all went straight to the hospital." She sighed. "Just like we're doing today."

Maddy was quiet for a few minutes. Asia opened her window and let the hot air blow on her face. She thought about the rest of the story. The doctor had kept Ira in the hospital for a week. Three-year-old Asia and her mother had stayed at Cold Creek to help Maddy. There were still a few cattle left and the garden to harvest. And when Ira came home, as good as new except for a pair of crutches, there was all the firewood to cut for the winter. One thing led to another.

Maddy offered Sherri and Asia their son Harry's old bedroom at the top of the house. Maddy washed the curtains and put quilts on the four-poster bed, made up a little cot for Asia and the two of them moved in.

Ten months later, on a long hot day in August, Sherri left. She took one small bag and left the rest of her belongings, including Asia, behind. She sent one postcard from a town in Saskatchewan. When Asia was old enough to understand, Maddy read her the postcard. *I'm sorry, Maddy. I love you Asia, and I will come back to get you. Sherri.* But Sherri hadn't come back, and the only explanation Maddy could come up with was that Asia had been born too early in Sherri's life and that Sherri had never had a chance to finish growing up. Eventually, Maddy put the postcard away with Asia's birth certificate and medical card in a box in her dresser drawer.

"Where in the world are we now?" said Ira.

"Just coming down the hill to the road into town," said Asia. Her stomach tightened at the thought of traffic lights and cars.

"I think Asia is a driver sent from heaven, don't you?" Ira's voice broke off. His eyes blinked a few times and then closed.

Maddy sounded worried. "Be quiet now, and let our girl concentrate."

～

Asia drove smack through the middle of town, staring at all the familiar landmarks as if she had never seen them before: the Royal Movie Palace, the feed store, Cariboo

Curios, where Ira sold his boxes, the Blue Lotus Café with the Friday-night Chinese smorgasbord, the post office. Everything looked different from the driver's seat.

She managed three intersections, stopping carefully for the red lights, but at the fourth intersection something went wrong. Brakes squealed, a car horn blared, and someone rolled down a window and shouted. Asia hunched her shoulders and kept going. She glanced over her shoulder to see if Maddy had noticed, but Maddy was fanning Ira's gray face with a piece of torn feed sack.

Then a police car slid up on the passenger side.

Maddy noticed that. "Sit up as tall as you can and stare straight ahead," she advised.

The police car glided past and at the next corner, her heart thudding, Asia turned left into the hospital parking lot.

CHAPTER FIVE

Maddy and Asia waited in a small room with two rows of vinyl chairs, a vending machine and a stack of worn magazines on a round table. As the minutes ticked into hours, a nurse tried to persuade them to go to the cafeteria for a proper meal, but Maddy refused to budge from the spot where they had wheeled Ira away. She stared straight ahead while Asia thumbed through tattered *People* magazines and read over and over a poster called *Alcohol and Your Unborn Baby*.

Finally Asia got up and went for a short walk. The lights in the hallways were dimmed. A man pushing a broom yawned as he walked by. Two nurses leaned against the wall, their heads together, laughing. Asia forced back tears. How could they be joking around? Didn't they know about Ira?

She went back to the waiting room and slumped in a chair. The hands on the big round clock on the wall crept by with a jerky clicking sound. People came and went—a man with a screaming toddler, a teenager holding his wrist, one girl comforting another, whose face was bleeding.

After what felt like ten years, a doctor in a white coat breezed through a set of swinging doors. He squeezed Maddy's hand. "Your husband had a heart attack. He's stabilized, and I can let you see him for a few minutes. But just one visitor at a time until he gets stronger."

Maddy followed the doctor through the door. Asia gathered up the remains of their supper—Styrofoam cups, half-eaten muffins and torn cellophane wrappers—and dumped everything in the garbage can beside the vending machine. Then she got up and went for another walk. By the time she returned, Maddy was standing in the middle of the waiting room, looking lost.

A nurse hovered at Maddy's side. She looked at Asia with relief. "He'll sleep for hours now," she whispered, as if Ira were right there in the room. "It's important you get some rest too. Is there anywhere you could go?"

Asia shook her head, but she took Maddy outside. Lights from the Rainbow Motel blinked in the dark a little way down the road. It was the motel where they stayed every winter when Ira brought his boxes to sell at the Christmas Craft Fair. It would have to do.

The woman behind the desk remembered them. She peered at Maddy over the top of her pink glasses. "My poor dear, you can fill out the paper work later. Right now you need a bed."

The room was hot and stuffy. Asia pulled the bedspread and thin blanket off the bed by the window and slid under the sheet. She waited while Maddy splashed water in the bathroom, and then with a creak and a rustle settled into the other bed. The motel light cast a pale red glow through the thin curtains. She wished Maddy would say something.

She took a big breath. "Is Ira going to die?" Her words dangled in the dark space in front of her.

At first she didn't know if Maddy had heard. Then Maddy said, "Ira is too stubborn to die."

Asia smiled. She stretched her toes to the bottom of the bed. "Remember you said you saw an owl in the sun on that day when Ira cut his leg?" She tried sleepily to organize her thoughts. "You said you couldn't ask for a clearer sign of trouble. But the owl brought good luck too."

"Now how is that?" said Maddy.

"It brought *me*."

"Well, bless your heart. It did indeed."

The last thing Asia heard as she drifted into sleep was Maddy murmuring softly, "I must have been wrong about owls after all."

CHAPTER SIX

Miranda's husband, George, had made a cross out of thin boards, and he built a fence around Daisy's grave to keep out the cows. The fence had rotted years ago, disappearing into the long grass, and weeds smothered everything now. Sometimes Miranda found pieces of pale gray wood that broke apart in her fingers, but she was never sure whether they had been part of the cross or the fence.

Miranda could make the abandoned house and barn look like the well-kept farm that she had loved, but her little girl's grave always remained neglected. Anger welled inside her now as she toiled in the sun, tugging at the grass and tough nettles. She worked on the grave every time she came to Cold Creek, but she never made any progress. She knew that it was part of her punishment, and she mumbled over and over as she worked, "The truth…She has to know the truth."

Montgomery watched her, his tail flicking back and forth. Once he bounded away after a mouse, pouncing through the tall grass in a graceful arc, but he was back in a few minutes, rubbing against her arm and purring. Finally Miranda stood up, smoothing her long blue skirt with her hands. The sun was high in the cloudless sky, and the distant gray mountains shimmered in the heat. The golden grass rippled before her like waves. She felt a moment of dizziness. Then her head cleared, and her eyes were pulled back to the mountains.

Almost a hundred years ago, a stranger had ridden out of those mountains, down through the high meadow to their farm. He must have had a past, a life before Cold Creek, but she never knew what it was. He was a prospector looking for work. He came from nowhere.

She licked her lips and whispered his name. Ridley Blackmore. A sour taste rose in her throat. Her hands tightened into fists. She wouldn't think about him or his tiny daughter Beatrice. Not now. A numbing fatigue spread through her limbs. That was enough work on Daisy's grave for today. Wearily, she picked up Montgomery. She would water her flowers. They were wilting and dying in the hot sun. And then she would go inside her house to rest.

❧

In the afternoon, she walked over the hill and along the creek to the big gray shingle house where Maddy and Ira and Asia lived. She still thought of it as the new house, even though Ira had built it almost fifty years ago. When Miranda came back to Cold Creek, she always stayed close to the Old Farm. She had only been to the new house a few times.

Her heart raced as she approached the log bridge. It crossed the creek at a place where the banks were close together, and the water was deep and black. There were fish in the shadows. Years ago, Miranda had watched a little boy hang over the bridge with his fishing rod. Someone from the house called, "Harry!" and he pulled in his rod and trudged off.

She had wondered if the boy had known that he was standing on the site of a much older bridge. The old bridge had collapsed in the high waters and raging rain of the spring of 1915. If you knew where to look, you could still see a few chunks of rotten beams in the bank. Bones. The bones of the old bridge.

Miranda forced herself to step onto the bridge. She kept her eyes fixed on the new house. Her heart thudded, and for a second she felt dizzy and had to stop. She longed to turn back, to flee to the safety of the Old Farm. But she needed to find Asia. She took a deep breath. She would be fine as long as she didn't look at the black water. As long as she didn't let herself remember.

Her steps quickened as she stepped off the bridge. She sensed right away that the place was deserted. She peered in the windows of the house and the workshop, and she checked the vegetable garden and the chicken coop. The sheep moved restlessly, and the hens set up a wild clucking.

She looked in the garage. The pickup truck was there, but the old white van was missing.

Tires crunched on the gravel driveway. A red truck bounced around the bend in the road and stopped in front of the house. An older man in blue jeans and a plaid shirt got out. She watched him toss a bale of hay to the sheep and throw corn for the chickens. Then he opened the front door of the house and disappeared inside.

He must be a neighbor, she thought. Her disappointment was a physical ache. The old couple and the girl had gone away, and she had no way of knowing when they would be back.

May 25, 1915

George has hired Blackmore to help him with the cattle. He says the man has experience with animals and is a hard worker.

Beatrice stays in the house with me during the day. She is a dear little girl, content to play for hours with the buttons from my button box. She speaks a little now, but only simple words like milk and kitty. She and Montgomery have become friends, although she was timid with him at first.

We had some sun this afternoon, and Beatrice and I went for a walk in the meadow. We picked a bouquet of lupines for Daisy's grave. I have never seen the creek so high. You can hear the water roaring even when you are inside the house. George says that if this wet spring continues there is a real danger the creek will flood its banks.

The nights are unseasonably cold, and this morning I urged Blackmore to let Beatrice sleep in the house. George is being very difficult about it, but I don't care.

I have put Beatrice in Daisy's bedroom, in her little pink bed.

CHAPTER SEVEN

"Harry is coming tomorrow," said Maddy. "You think Ira is stubborn, you wait until you meet Harry."

"I thought he wasn't coming until Thanksgiving," said Asia. "And besides, he always says he's coming, but he never has."

"His life is too hectic, that's the problem," said Maddy. "He does try, but something always prevents him at the last minute. But this time, he's coming for sure."

Asia's stomach tightened. That meant that Harry must be really worried about Ira.

She and Maddy were having supper in the café attached to the motel. Asia had eaten most of her meals by herself for the past three days, charging them to their room, while Maddy lived on muffins and sat with Ira. That afternoon, Ira had smiled at Maddy and squeezed her hand with some of his old strength, and Maddy relaxed a little and joined Asia for a bowl of soup.

Asia mulled over the idea of Harry coming while she nibbled on French fries. In a photograph in the living room at Cold Creek he looked about fourteen, and he was wearing coveralls and a floppy hat just like Ira's. He was standing beside the dark pool under the bridge, grinning and holding up a big trout. When Christmas cards and birthday cards arrived with hastily scrawled messages from Harry, Asia always pictured the boy in the coveralls. It was hard to connect him with the grown-up Harry who worked for a computer company and had lived in Hong Kong with his wife, Joyce, for the past ten years.

Asia thought about the blue airmail letter with Hong Kong stamps that had arrived at the end of May. Maddy had read bits out loud to Ira and Asia on the porch after supper. Harry's time in Hong Kong was over and the company was sending him back.

"Back to Cold Creek?" Asia asked, trying to imagine sharing Maddy and Ira with a stranger.

"Back to Southern California," said Maddy. "That's what Harry means. His company's head office is there." The thin sheets of paper rustled in her hands. "Harry and Joyce will be in California by the middle of July, and they're coming here for Thanksgiving weekend."

They sat in silence for a few minutes, and then Ira said, "I hope he doesn't try to stir things up. He knows, doesn't he?"

"Of course he knows," said Maddy. Her voice sounded strained.

"Well, I just hope he doesn't make trouble."

Asia looked at Ira curiously. "What does Harry know? Trouble about what?" she asked, but Maddy shot Ira a warning look and folded the letter and put it back in the envelope.

None of it made much sense to Asia. For awhile, she wondered if they were worried that Harry would mind that she had his old bedroom. That was all she could come up with, and it was silly when you thought about it. Harry was an adult. Still, something was making Maddy and Ira anxious. But Thanksgiving was ages away, and after a few days Asia forgot all about it.

And now Harry was coming tomorrow instead. Asia pushed away her plate. She had always thought it would be impossible to get sick of fries and gravy. "When will he get here?" she said.

"His plane gets into Vancouver early in the morning. He's renting a car and will be here right after lunch." Maddy sighed. "Harry is a fast driver."

Asia spun the sugar bowl in a circle. "I wonder what Harry will think of me."

Maddy stirred three sugar cubes into her tea. "Well, he'll like you a lot," she said.

Asia thought she saw a tiny flash of fear in Maddy's eyes. Her mind drifted back to the peculiar conversation between Ira and Maddy the day Harry's letter came. She must be imagining things. How could Maddy be afraid of her own son? And what did that have to do with Asia?

～

The elder Hildebrands visited Ira at the hospital in the morning. Anna and Katya stayed with Asia in the motel room, eating sugary slices of their grandmother's home-baked apple strudel and watching TV.

"Is it fun living in a motel?" said Katya, bouncing on the bed.

"It's okay," said Asia. "The best part is I get to charge anything I want at the cafe."

She showed Katya all the things that Maddy had bought at the drugstore because they had left Cold Creek in such a hurry—the tiny bottles of shampoo and conditioner, the travel toothbrushes and the miniature tubes of toothpaste that folded up together, her two new T-shirts.

The Hildebrands came back to the motel to take the girls out for lunch, and then left for home. The room felt empty and lonely without Katya's bubbly laugh. Asia flicked through TV channels for awhile and then wandered over to the hospital to find Maddy. Each time Asia visited Ira, her heart thumped when she saw his pale gray face and the tubes taped to his sunken chest.

Maddy was dozing in a chair in the corner. Asia sat beside the bed and held Ira's hand and watched the blinks on the monitor. After a long time, a loud voice and heavy footsteps sounded in the hallway outside the door. A tanned man in a beige suit swept into the room.

Maddy stood up. "Harry!"

He was taller than Asia expected. He crushed Maddy in a huge hug. "You look wonderful, Mother. You don't look any different at all."

"I wish that were true," said Maddy, but she was beaming. She held his hand tightly. "Ten years is a long time, Harry."

"Too long," said Harry.

He looked at Asia, and she realized she had been staring. She felt her cheeks redden. "This is Asia," said Maddy.

There was a moment of silence. It felt to Asia as if a heavy dark cloud of disapproval had entered the room. But how could Harry disapprove of her when he didn't even know her? Then Harry smiled and said brightly, "I've brought everyone gifts from Hong Kong. They're in my suitcase."

"That's lovely," said Maddy.

A movement came from Ira's bed. He struggled awake, blinking in confusion.

"Give him a minute," said Maddy. She patted Ira's arm and said quietly, "Harry's here, Ira. Harry's come home."

Ira licked his dry lips. "Let me see him," he said in a tremulous voice.

Harry took Asia's chair beside the bed. He waited while Ira sipped some water, and then plunged into a story about some mix-up over his flight.

There was too much Harry. He filled the whole room. Asia decided the photograph in the living room at Cold Creek must be a mistake. This couldn't possibly be the boy with the grin and the fish. She drifted to the window and watched a poodle and a golden retriever playing on the lawn in front of the hospital. Maddy's knitting needles clicked softly beside her. She'd knitted a few rows every day since she'd read in a magazine that the gentle movement might help her arthritis.

A nurse came in and adjusted the curtains. "Two more minutes, that's all." Her face was set.

"I want to talk to you about my father's medication," said Harry, following her out of the room. Maddy and Asia found him a few minutes later, leaning over the counter at the nurse's station, deep in conversation.

Harry rented a room at the Rainbow Motel next to Maddy and Asia's. They had dinner in the café. Maddy and Asia ordered the special—hamburger steak with mashed potatoes—but Harry said it was too hot for hamburger and asked for a house salad.

"Mother," he said, while they waited for their order, "what's this I hear about an onion under Father's bed?"

Uh-oh, thought Asia. She busied herself with folding and unfolding her napkin.

"Everyone knows that a cut onion under a sick person's bed will help him get better faster," said Maddy.

"Everyone doesn't know that. Just you, it seems. The nurse told me there was an odd smell every time she went into the room, and she was not happy when she found the onion."

Asia sipped her ice water and peeked at Maddy. Maddy had set her chin. She could be just as stubborn as Ira when she needed to be. "That nurse doesn't know twiddle," she said.

Harry leaned forward. "And you have to stop pestering the nurses about moving Father's bed. It's ridiculous."

"You can insist all you like, but a bed facing north and south brings bad luck." This time Maddy's voice faltered, and Asia realized with a pang that Harry was wearing her down.

Was this what Ira meant when he said he hoped Harry wouldn't stir things up, wouldn't cause trouble? Asia had a queasy feeling that there were lots of things about Harry she didn't know yet.

The meals came and Asia picked at her food, only half listening to Harry's stories of Hong Kong. She sighed. When you thought about it, eating in restaurants was very over-rated. What she really wanted was to go home.

CHAPTER EIGHT

"A condo—what?" said Ira.

"A condominium," said Harry. "You know what that is. Don't pretend, Pop."

Sometime in the last few days, Harry had stopped calling Maddy and Ira Mother and Father. He looked different too. Asia had just come back to Ira's room from the motel, and she studied Harry from the doorway. He hadn't shaved, and he was wearing jeans and an old denim shirt.

Harry looked unhappy to see Asia. "I think we should talk about this later."

"No," said Maddy. "Finish what you started to say."

Harry hesitated for a second, then plunged ahead. "We live in a great town. You'll love it. I know you will. There's all kinds of things to do."

Asia stared at Harry. He wanted them to go to California? Leave Cold Creek?

Harry stood up and paced around the room. "Joyce wants you to come," he said. Maddy stared at him in disbelief. "She'd love to have you. The condo is too big for us. There's lots of room."

"It's a very generous offer," said Maddy, "but no thank you."

"I'm not saying you wouldn't ever come back here," said Harry. "Think of it as migrating."

Ira looked bewildered. Harry ploughed on. "I've given this a lot of thought. Winters in California, summers at Cold Creek. Lots of people your age do that. They call them snowbirds."

Maddy laughed, and Harry frowned at her.

"Why do we need to go to California?" said Ira. "I'm getting better. No more tubes soon."

"Yes, you are getting better," said Harry slowly. Asia thought he sounded like he was talking to a child. "But you and Mama both heard the doctor. You can't go back to Cold Creek. It's not an option, Pop. Not in the winter. You've only got that woodstove for heat, and sometimes it's days before the road gets plowed. And Mama can't do the work anymore."

"How do you know all that?" said Maddy.

"I just do." Harry turned back to Ira. "Besides, the warm winter in Southern California would be the best thing for Mama's arthritis. The doctor explained that too. She needs a change of climate."

Ira's face sagged. Asia could feel him weakening. How could he deny that Maddy needed some relief?

Harry must have sensed the change in Ira. "I'm just asking you to think about it. Both of you. We don't have to decide anything today."

Ira turned to Asia. "So what do you say, chickadee? How would you like to fly to California for the winter?"

Harry coughed. "I said we shouldn't discuss this right now. But you might as well know. We'd have to make other arrangements for Asia. It's an adults-only condominium."

The room filled with a terrible silence.

"What kind of condominium?" said Ira finally.

"An adults-only condominium," repeated Harry.

"I never heard of such a thing," said Maddy, as if Harry had made it up.

Harry looked uncomfortable. "You can't have children there. But I'm sure we can make arrangements for Asia. What about the Hildebrands? Or maybe she could stay with a family closer to town so she could go to school. Remember, this is not forever."

Anger and fear surged through Asia. Maddy and Ira were her family. How dare Harry talk about her as if she weren't there? How dare he make plans for her life?

"Go to California without my angel?" exclaimed Ira. "Who would save me if I had another heart attack?"

Harry glanced nervously at the door. "Don't shout, Pop. You're going to get all the nurses running in. You're not *going* to have another heart attack. That's the whole point of this."

"And I'm not going to California or any dang place without Asia," said Ira.

"Of course not," said Maddy. She picked up her knitting. "Ira, do you think it's time to look for a new puppy?"

Harry's face closed. Asia knew he would not give up easily.

Asia thought back over the summer. She had been careful with ladybugs. She had found a four-leaf clover behind Ira's workshop, and had removed one of the eggs when the hens laid an even number. She had done everything right. Why was this happening to them?

Harry had come without signs, like a big wind blowing into their lives, and in the end she knew he was going to ruin everything.

CHAPTER NINE

"You told me she was a foster child," said Harry.

Asia froze. She had wandered down to the motel office to buy a can of Coke and was on her way back to their room to watch TV. Harry's door wasn't quite closed, and his voice carried onto the walkway. Maddy was in there too. A chair creaked, and she murmured something in reply.

"No, it's not the same thing," said Harry. There was an edge of anger in his voice. "It's not the same thing at all. I had no idea. It changes everything."

"What does it change?" said Maddy, her voice stronger. "Even if Asia *were* a foster child, did you really think we'd just send her off to another family?"

There was a long silence. A TV blared from another room, and a car door slammed. Finally Harry said, "Asia must have some real family somewhere."

Asia pressed herself against the wall. Maddy and Ira were her real family.

"There's no one," said Maddy. "Sherri told us that Asia's father was never part of the picture. She said her own parents were dead and she had no brothers or sisters. She never talked about anyone else."

"Yes, but you just told me that Sherri showed up out of nowhere, looking for some commune, stayed ten months and then abandoned her daughter. I'm sorry, Mama, that doesn't make me inclined to believe her."

Asia hugged her arms to her chest. Harry was wrong, wrong about everything.

"Well," said Maddy after a pause, "if Sherri had family, she kept it a secret."

"Friends then? Didn't she have any friends?"

"Sherri had nobody except us," said Maddy. "You didn't know her. She'd had a hard time, I could tell. A terrible time. She found some happiness at Cold Creek."

"You don't expect me to feel sorry for her?"

"I don't expect you to feel anything, Harry. And I'm not trying to make excuses for what she did."

"So Sherri just dropped in out of the blue. No past, no family, nothing."

"More or less."

"And she left the same way, only she didn't take her daughter."

There was a pause, and then Maddy said, "Sherri met someone in town. His name was Ted. I don't know his last name. She talked about him a lot. She got a job waitressing at one of the restaurants in town, and he used to come in for coffee."

"She took off with some guy she hardly knew? A man she picked up in a restaurant?"

"I think she just wanted to have a little break, a fling." Maddy sounded exhausted. "She took a few clothes and left everything else here. I'm certain she meant to come back. It wasn't right, but she did it. Sometimes, Harry, good people do bad things."

Asia could hear Harry walking back and forth. He lowered his voice a little. "You must have been in shock. Sherri was gone and you were stuck with her three-year-old daughter."

"Not stuck," said Maddy. "Oh no. Never stuck. We love Asia, and as hard as you may find this to believe, we loved Sherri."

"So after she left, you thought it was okay to just keep Asia without telling anybody."

"For a long time we waited for Sherri to come back. When we finally realized she wasn't going to, it was too late. How could we even think of letting Asia go then?"

"So why didn't you try to make it legal? If you're so sure there's no family, why didn't you apply to be her foster parents?"

"Because we were afraid the child welfare people would say no. Because we're too old. And we don't live near a school. And then they would have taken her away and given her to strangers."

"Didn't people ever ask any questions? And what about school?"

"She gets her lessons in the mail. Just like you did."

Harry grunted.

"We have her birth certificate, her medical card. If anyone ever asked, we said she was our granddaughter."

"That's not the point," said Harry. "You could have used the birth certificate to trace her family."

"I told you, Sherri said she had no family. And we would have lost Asia." For the first time, Asia heard fear in Maddy's voice. After a long silence Maddy said, "What are you going to do?"

"I don't know," said Harry. "But I have to do something. We know Asia's last name is Cumfrey. I'll look in the Vancouver phone book and see how many Cumfreys are listed."

"Sherri wasn't from Vancouver." Maddy's voice was crumbling into uncertainty. "She said she grew up in the United States."

"Well, it's a place to start. It would help if we had a little more information."

Asia squeezed her eyes shut. Harry was going to send her away. He was going to send her away to live with strangers. "Make him stop, Maddy," she whispered. "*Please*, make him stop."

But Maddy just said quietly, "Why do you have to do this, Harry?"

Maddy was afraid. Asia didn't want to hear any more. She slipped back to their room and crawled under the clammy sheets. Her arms and legs felt icy.

Maddy came in a few minutes later. Asia lay very still and pretended to be asleep. She couldn't bear to talk to her right now. She couldn't understand why Maddy hadn't told Harry to leave them alone.

CHAPTER TEN

Asia slid into a chair at a table in the corner of the café. Her legs ached like she had the flu, and she had been too tired to brush her hair, yanking it into an untidy ponytail instead. Harry was concentrating on a plate of sausages and eggs, and he grunted a good morning without looking up, but Maddy put down her cup of tea and smiled at her. Asia pretended not to notice.

Harry poured ketchup on his eggs. It was gross. Asia bit back her anger. How could he just sit there stuffing himself as if nothing had happened? And Maddy was sipping her tea like everything was normal. She peeked at Maddy's face. She looked pale, but otherwise the same as always. Asia had a sudden wild hope that she had dreamed all that stuff that Harry had said about finding her real family.

"Orange juice, sleepy head?" said the waitress. Asia nodded. The waitress's name was Skye, and she had been friendly to Asia all week and very sympathetic about Ira. Asia studied Skye's fingernails while she poured the juice. They were perfect purple ovals.

"I'll have Fruit Loops too, please," she said. Maddy didn't allow her to have sugary cereals, and she waited for her to object. But Maddy didn't say anything. She didn't even seem to have noticed.

Asia watched Skye wipe down the table next to theirs and then carry a stack of dirty plates to the kitchen. Why hadn't Maddy ever told her that Sherri had been a waitress, wiping tables and taking orders just like Skye? Maybe she had even worked *here*. For a second she pretended that Skye was her mother, which was stupid because Sherri hadn't looked at all like Skye. Asia had never seen a picture of her mother, and she didn't remember her, but Maddy had told her that Sherri had long black hair too. It was one of the few things she did know.

Asia stared at the bowl of Fruit Loops that Skye set in front of her. They had a sickly perfume smell that she secretly loathed. She caught the tail end of Harry's announcement. "...absolutely forbid Asia to drive the van. It's highly illegal."

"Where are we going?" she said, breaking her vow to never talk to Harry again.

"Home," said Maddy. "I think we've had enough of motel life."

"Ira too?" said Asia quickly.

"Not yet. But Harry has reorganized his schedule, so he can stay until Ira is better. He'll drive us in every day."

"Oh," said Asia.

"I've arranged for a man from the gas station to bring the van out on the weekend." Harry stood up. "I've got to go back to the motel room to make a few more phone calls, and then I'll square up the bill."

Asia opened her mouth to argue about the van and then changed her mind. She waited until Harry had left and said, "How long is he going to stay with us?"

"That depends on Ira," said Maddy. "Harry has always been good at arranging and organizing. That's a point in his favor."

Maddy put Harry in the small spare bedroom at the back of the house. Within a few hours of their return to Cold Creek, his presence was everywhere. His briefcase and papers took up most of the big pine table, his laptop and printer bleeped in the living room, and his abandoned mugs of coffee turned up in unexpected places.

Asia loved their big house, with its old woodstove, worn floors, braided rugs and shelves full of books. It made her furious when Harry stopped suddenly in front of the wringer washing machine and said, "I can't believe you still use this." A few minutes later, he stared at the windup record player and laughed. "Don't tell me you still have this old thing?"

Maddy took one look at Asia's face and sent her to the garden to pick vegetables for supper.

The garden overlooked the creek and was surrounded by a weathered gray fence to keep the deer out. Asia always thought it was a little bit like the secret garden in one of her favorite books. Maddy grew vegetables and flowers all mixed together, daisies behind the carrots, rows of marigolds and beets, an old barrel full of poppies in the middle of the potato patch. As Maddy put it, nothing was expected to behave in any particular way. Squash vines crept into the lettuce, huge sunflowers towered over the zucchini, and scarlet runner beans trailed along the fence.

Asia went to the raspberry patch at the end of the garden and chased away two sparrows pecking on the fruit. She feasted on berries for a few minutes and then wandered up and down the rows, lingering and letting the spell of Maddy's garden soothe her. She picked carrots, some of the last late peas, a golden zucchini and a curly red lettuce, and then carried everything into the kitchen.

Harry was leaning against the wall while Maddy stirred custard on the stove. She had declared that they would have a good homemade meal tonight, and the kitchen was filled with the smell of roasting pork. Asia sniffed appreciatively, and then noticed Harry's face. He looked highly annoyed. "I can't get any cell phone reception here at all."

Maddy took the basket from Asia and dumped the vegetables into the sink. "Use the radiophone," she suggested.

"That's ridiculous. There's no way I can talk to clients on a radiophone." Harry's voice rose. "It makes them nervous. All the starting and stopping. Mama, this is just one more reason—"

Maddy frowned at Harry and his voice trailed off. He was going to talk about California again. Asia's heart thudded. California, where Joyce could help with Ira, and Maddy's arthritis would get better. California, where the condominium had a stupid rule that said no kids.

"Tell me about Joyce's new art class," said Maddy, and Asia slipped out the door. She went straight to her climbing tree, the big old pine beside the creek. Ira had nailed three thin boards for steps at the bottom where there were no branches. Asia climbed up them, and then scrambled from branch to branch, going higher and deeper into the cool green world of her tree. The bark scratched her bare legs and pine needles dropped into her hair, but her heart slowed as she pushed away thoughts of California and concentrated on climbing. When she reached her favorite spot, where a thick limb made a kind of seat, she leaned back against the trunk and breathed in big gulps of pine-scented air.

Maddy was nervous about all Asia's climbing—up trees and along high fence rails and on top of the huge round bales of hay—but Ira said Asia was a born climber and nothing would stop her. He built the steps because she was going to climb that old pine anyway. Also, he said, everyone needed a place to go to think about things. He had his workshop, Maddy had the garden and Asia had her tree.

When Asia was little, she thought she could see the whole world from her tree. Now she knew it was just a tiny piece, but she still loved the view. She was eye to eye with the black rooster weathervane on the peak of their house, and she looked down on the mossy shingled roofs of Ira's workshop, the hen house and the sheep barn. Or she could look across the creek, past the log bridge, to the meadows and the distant mountains. One day, Asia planned to climb right to the very top of the tree to find out if she could see all the way to the Old Farm.

Harry was walking across the bridge now, his cell phone swinging in his hand. Asia watched him and wondered if he had found the black beetle she had slipped into his shoe for bad luck. He left the creek and started trudging up the slope of the high meadow. Every few minutes he stopped and waved the phone above his head.

Asia grinned. Harry was trying to get reception. She hoped he would have to climb all the way to the top of the meadow in the broiling hot sun. Suddenly something stirred in the grass to the right of him. Asia held her breath as the long low body of a coyote trotted in Harry's direction. For a second, the man and the coyote were intent on their own paths. Then the coyote spotted Harry and froze.

Harry was an intruder in the coyote's meadow. Asia knew how the coyote felt. She waited to see what it would do. Harry, oblivious to the coyote's presence, continued slogging his way up the slope, and after a minute the coyote turned back the way it had come, its gray-brown coat blending into the grass.

Asia sighed and looked back at Harry. He had stopped walking, and she wondered if he had finally got his phone to work. She wished he would stay there. She wished he would talk to his clients all night.

~

After supper, Maddy suggested they all go for a walk to the Old Farm. Harry was keen, and he dug Ira's fishing rod and tackle box out of the cupboard. "I might as well make a few casts while we're there," he said. "There's a great spot right below the old house. It never failed when I was a kid."

Asia stared at Harry. She still couldn't believe that he had actually lived at Cold Creek. She hated watching him sort through the fishing flies, all carefully tied by Ira, picking out the ones he wanted. Harry had no right to touch them. They were Ira's.

She walked slowly, so Maddy would know that she didn't want to go. But Maddy was listening to Harry's chatter with a faint smile on her face, and she didn't even notice when Asia lingered on the bridge to drop stones in the water. Didn't Maddy know that Harry was the enemy? Asia sighed. She would have to be on guard for both of them.

She watched one of her stones make ripples in the dark water and shivered. Even on a hot day, a pocket of cold air hung over the log bridge. Ira said there was a scientific explanation, something about low spots and cross drafts. Maddy had listened politely and then nailed a horseshoe on the end of one of the logs. Asia threw her last stone into the water and hopped off the bridge. She followed Harry and Maddy across the meadow, her steps just quick enough to keep them in sight.

CHAPTER ELEVEN

The weeds were stubborn, and Miranda's back ached from bending over Daisy's grave. She found more of the faded gray boards from the old fence and stacked them in a neat pile to one side. As she worked, a small icy core of doubt grew inside her. She had been so sure that Asia had heard her speak, but now she wondered if she had made a mistake.

She went over and over in her mind what had happened at the dog's grave. *Too much death,* she had said, and the girl had glanced around. Had there been a breeze that day? Was that what Asia sensed, nothing more than the wind playing in the aspen trees? She straightened and rubbed her shoulders. No matter how hard she worked, Daisy's grave still looked so abandoned. Surely those weeds had not been there yesterday. And the grass was persistent, smothering overnight the spot that she had cleared.

The sun was low in the sky. It was the end of another long day. For a few minutes, Miranda thought longingly of her other home. Her home beside the sea. It was easier there, the memories kinder. She sighed. She had worked too hard today. It was time to go inside her house and put the kettle on for tea, perhaps play her piano.

Montgomery was beside the creek, watching minnows dart about in the dark water, and she called to him. Unwillingly, her eyes flickered to a wide flat spot on the bank. Ridley Blackmore had camped there for almost a month. Sometimes she thought she could still see his canvas tent and smell the smoke from his fire.

George had hired Blackmore as a ranch hand, and for the first week the two men had worked side by side in silence. Then George started taking his coffee with Blackmore after supper, and Miranda could see their shadows by the campfire and hear the murmur of their voices long after dusk. At the time she hadn't cared, because it meant that she and the little girl Beatrice were alone in the evenings, but now she wondered what they talked about, night after night. The war that was pulling men away from their families and ranches? The price of cattle? The new road that was opening up the Cariboo?

Montgomery bunted against her leg. Miranda shook her troubling thoughts away, and picked him up and carried him inside the house. She paused beside the woodstove.

Voices drifted through the soft evening air, and for a second she was confused and thought that George and Blackmore were coming in for their supper. But how could that be? They had been dead for almost a hundred years. She walked to the window and peered outside. Her breath caught in her throat. The voices belonged to Maddy and Asia and a strange man. They were walking down the hill above the Old Farm.

Asia was back! Miranda frowned. It would be so much easier if Asia were alone. She hesitated and then fled up the stairs, slipping into a little room off the landing. She couldn't hear the voices now, but she knew the people were coming. She pressed her hands against her dress and waited.

CHAPTER TWELVE

When Asia walked over the hill and looked down at the barn and the old house, her dark mood slipped away. She loved the Old Farm, especially in the evenings when the sun turned everything a soft mellow brown. The buildings sagged into the ground, their roofs covered in silvery-green moss. Maddy had told Asia that when she and Ira first came to Cold Creek, there were traces of an old garden around the house. She had found patches of lavender, mint and yarrow. But the nettles and weeds had taken over, and although Asia had hunted, the flowers had disappeared.

Nobody knew very much about the people who had lived at the Old Farm. When Asia was ten, Edna Finster, the curator at the museum in town, had unearthed a hand-lettered poster advertising an auction at Cold Creek on Saturday, June 29, 1915.

Maddy took Ira and Asia to the museum to see it. The paper had yellowed but you could still read the faded print. It listed all the things at the Cold Creek farm that were for sale—the hay rake, the mower, the shorthorn cattle and the furniture from the house.

"Look!" Asia had said. "There's even a piano for sale!"

"*Sale by owners George and Miranda Williams,*" Maddy read.

"They weren't planning on coming back," said Ira in a wondering voice. "Why would anyone want to leave Cold Creek?"

"Edna said it was probably the war," said Maddy. "All the young men were leaving their ranches and signing up. But I have a notion it was something else."

～

Every time she went to the Old Farm, Asia thought about the people who had lived there. George and Miranda Williams. She decided that George was sensible, with a big handlebar mustache. Miranda was beautiful. Her hair was thick and the color of honey. She roamed the meadows and fields of Cold Creek like a wild deer, singing and picking armfuls of flowers. In the evenings, she played the piano for George, who was madly in love with her. And Maddy was wrong. It *was* the war that separated them. Asia had a vivid picture in her mind of Miranda crying on the platform of the train station, while George waved bravely from a window.

"Could Miranda and George still be alive today?" she had asked Maddy.

"Oh no," said Maddy. "They must have been adults when they lived at Cold Creek—in their twenties at least. That would mean they would have to be, let's see, at least one hundred and fifteen. And of course, they might have been much older. They might have been as old as Ira and me."

Asia preferred to imagine the beautiful young Miranda and her adoring husband. She ran ahead of Maddy and Harry and stood in the doorway of the old house and gazed around. It was one big room with a staircase in the middle. Except for an old black woodstove, it was empty. Dry leaves were scattered across the old floorboards and had blown into piles in the corners. Swallows had swooped through the open windows and built mud nests in the beams, their pale droppings and a few downy feathers spattered on the stove.

Asia wished she could see the house the way it used to be. She liked imagining where George and Miranda had put their furniture. Did they have a table by the window? Where had the piano stood? Where did they sit in the evenings? There were some old cupboards with peeled blue paint on one wall, and Asia had found treasures in them: a skinny brown bottle, an oddly shaped piece of metal and an old-fashioned lady's boot.

She poked around behind the stove for a few minutes, and then looked longingly at the sagging staircase. She was absolutely forbidden to go on even the first step. It was one of Ira's firmest rules. He said the stairs were rotten and likely to collapse at any time, but Asia knew if she could only get up there, she would find all kinds of wonderful things.

Suddenly a gray shape slipped through the shadows at the top of the staircase. Asia froze.

Me-rooow.

The cry made her jump, and then she let out her breath with a whoosh. It was just a cat. But how would a stray cat get all the way to the Old Farm? There were no cats at Cold Creek because they made Maddy uneasy. The nearest cat was Buster, who belonged to the Hildebrands, but they lived almost two miles away. And besides, Buster was orange with faded black stripes.

"Here, kitty," she called. "Here, kitty, kitty."

The house was silent now, but she knew she hadn't imagined the cry. There was a cat upstairs and she would love to find it. She glanced back toward the door. Ever since Harry had come, Maddy hardly paid any attention to her. She was probably with Harry now, watching him cast his fishing line in the creek. She glanced up the stairs again and then rested her foot on the first step. It didn't feel rotten; it was firm and not at all wobbly. Her mind made up, she started to climb. She tested each step before she put her weight on it, but not one of them felt like it was going to cave in. Ira had been worrying for nothing.

At the top of the staircase, Asia stood still for a minute, her heart beating fast. Two closed doors faced a small landing. There was no sign of the cat. She frowned. How could it have completely disappeared like that? She opened one of the doors and peered into a small bare room. There was one dusty window with a missing pane of glass, and the floor was covered in dirt and dry brown leaves. No treasures in there. She turned to the other door, which opened with a soft creak.

She sucked in her breath and stared in amazement at a little bed with a curved pink wooden headboard, a narrow pink chest of drawers and a rocking chair. Why hadn't Maddy and Ira ever told her about this? Asia always imagined that George and Miranda Williams had lived at the Old Farm by themselves. She never imagined children. But this room had obviously belonged to a little girl. She stepped inside and walked over to the bed. On the faded headboard, pale purple and yellow flowers and a name were faintly visible. She traced the ornate letters with her fingers and said out loud, "Daisy."

CHAPTER THIRTEEN

There was a muffled sound behind Asia, like a soft footstep on a wooden floorboard. The cat! she thought as she spun around.

There was nothing there. But the rocking chair was moving gently back and forth, as if someone had been sitting in it and had just stood up. She stared at it and then called, "Where are you, kitty?"

Her loud voice in the silent house startled her. There was no answering *meow*. The cat must have jumped on the rocking chair and then somehow vanished again. She glanced around uneasily. The chair was still now, but there was something weird about the room. It was ridiculous, but it felt as if someone else were there.

She walked over to the window, rubbed a clean patch in the middle of the glass and peered outside. Maddy was sitting on the bank beside the creek, her white hair like a dandelion puff in the sun. Harry had given up on fishing and was striding toward the old barn, calling something over his shoulder that made Maddy laugh. Asia took a deep breath. She was letting the old house scare her.

She turned around and hesitated, frowning. Then she knelt in front of the dresser and tugged at the top drawer. It stuck for a minute and then opened with a jerk. It was full of clothes: little socks that looked hand knitted and white cotton slips and undershirts, all neatly folded. She opened the other drawers and one by one she lifted out tiny dresses made of soft pastel fabrics. Most of the dresses were plain, but there was one pale yellow dress with an embroidered yoke that must have been for Sunday best.

Asia rocked back on her heels. She stared at the bed and imagined the little girl who had slept in it. Daisy. She was pretty like her mother, Miranda, Asia decided. She loved Cold Creek and cried buckets when they sold everything at the auction and moved away. Asia wouldn't cry if she and Maddy and Ira had to leave Cold Creek. She wouldn't give Harry the satisfaction. She stood up and took one more glance around. Was it possible that Maddy and Ira didn't know about all the things in this room? I might be the only person who's been up here for almost a hundred years, she thought with a shiver.

She had the eerie sensation again that someone was in the room with her. Only this time it was much stronger. A whisper of icy air washed over her bare legs. There was a rustling noise that sounded like a long skirt brushing against the floor. Something touched her arm.

Asia screamed and ran out of the room and down the stairs, the blood pounding in her ears. She jumped off the last step and stumbled across the room to the front door.

"Wait," said a voice behind her. "Please, don't be frightened. Don't go."

Asia spun around. Something hovered in the middle of the staircase. It drifted in and out of focus, the edges blurred like a reflection in water. For a second, the form became clear. It was a young woman, wearing a long blue dress with a shawl over her shoulders. Her face was an indistinct pale oval and although Asia couldn't see her lips, the voice came again. "Please stay."

The woman floated toward her. Asia turned and raced outside into the soft sunlight. Maddy was walking up from the creek toward the house. Asia stood frozen until Maddy was beside her.

Maddy gave her a sharp look. "Are you all right?"

Asia couldn't tell Maddy—not now. She would be in terrible trouble for going up the old stairs. Besides, Harry was coming back from the barn, calling to them cheerfully. He would laugh or, even worse, say she was making it up. Her throat felt dry, and she swallowed. "I'm fine," she whispered.

Harry was full of enthusiasm. "That old rope I swung on is still there. Do you remember, Mama, right off the peak of the roof like Tarzan?"

"Well, I hope you don't have any ideas about trying it again," said Maddy with a laugh.

Asia's head spun with confusion as they started up the hill toward home. Suddenly, in the distance, the haunting notes of a piano drifted through the soft summer evening. The sound was coming from the old house. She stood still. Harry was still talking about the barn, and neither he nor Maddy looked back. The music was all around her now, and she knew that it was the woman she had seen on the stairs. She had never heard anyone play like that before. The music brimmed with both joy and sadness.

There is no piano in the house, but she is playing one, thought Asia. And I am the only one who can hear it. She looked back at the Old Farm, with a mixture of shock and excitement.

~

Miranda's fingers flew over the piano keys. This time Asia had seen her. She was positive. She winced when she remembered how the girl had screamed. Asia was terrified of her—Miranda should have expected that. She glanced at Montgomery, who was washing himself in a patch of evening sun. "What a good boy, Montgomery," she murmured. "You helped, didn't you? You led her to Daisy's room."

Miranda knew that Asia hadn't seen the gleaming piano, the sturdy furniture that George had built, the bright braid rugs. She was pretty sure that all she saw was a dirty floor, bare walls and broken windows. It was a shame. But Asia *had* seen the things in Daisy's room. She had looked so surprised.

Maddy and Ira never saw anything she did in her house. Over the years they poked their heads in now and again, and once she heard Ira say, "These stairs don't look at all safe to me. I better board them off; there's nothing up there anyway, just a couple of empty rooms." He never got around to it, but it was the last time he had gone upstairs.

Why had Asia been able to see the things in Daisy's room but not the rest of the house? Miranda's fingers trembled on the piano keys. She had thought of little else but Daisy since she had returned to the Old Farm. Her little girl's presence was so strong. Asia must have felt it too.

It had taken all of Miranda's energy to let Asia see her, and she was exhausted. But it had been worth it. Her connection with Asia was growing stronger, and she was certain now Asia was the one who could help her. For a few blissful moments, Miranda bent over the keys of her piano and lost herself completely in her beloved music.

May 29, 1915

I stayed up for three nights making Beatrice a doll. I sewed it from a piece of soft flannel, with two black buttons for eyes and a smiling mouth stitched out of pink embroidery floss. When I gave it to her, she hugged it tightly and her face broke into a wonderful smile. "Baby," she said. "Baby!"

It is Beatrice's second week at Cold Creek, and she says many words now. It seems that she only needed a little affection and encouragement to bring her out of herself. This morning she cried out "Papa!" when we met Blackmore on our morning walk. Her little voice was as clear and sweet as a bell, but if Blackmore was pleased he did not show it.

Beatrice and I have a secret. I told her that when we are alone, she may call me Mama. Beatrice looked at me over the rim of her mug with her sharp brown eyes, and I felt my heart thud in my chest. "Mama," she said. She smiled. Her teeth were like milky pearls.

Tears slid down my cheeks. I touched the little girl's hair. I washed it this morning in the tub by the woodstove, and I am delighted to see how it shines. Tomorrow I will put it in rags for curls.

June 5, 1915

George has told Blackmore that he cannot afford to pay any more wages. At once the man made plans for a prospecting trip. This is not as terrible as it sounds because he is leaving Beatrice with us until his return in two weeks.

Beatrice gripped my hand tightly while we watched her father tie the ropes on his packhorse. George advised him that the creek is too high to ride across safely and that he would have to cross at the log bridge, about half a mile upstream.

Blackmore's horses stepped quickly through the meadow grass. Beatrice burst into tears, but the man rode away without a backward glance. George said he knew something that would distract her from her crying. He set Beatrice on a straight-backed chair on the porch and brought out his camera and took her photograph. At the last minute Montgomery jumped into her lap, and George said that he could be in the picture too. The camera is George's prized possession, but he has not brought it out since he took the photograph of Daisy, on her third birthday, a few days before she became ill.

CHAPTER FOURTEEN

The hardest part was keeping a secret from Maddy. They sat on the porch after supper and shelled late peas from the garden, Maddy in her rocking chair and Asia on the top step. Asia liked the sound of the crisp pea pods snapping open and the soft plop of the peas falling into the bowl.

She glanced at Maddy's bent head. If she decided to tell her what had happened at the Old Farm, she would be cross that Asia had disobeyed Ira, but Asia knew that she would believe her. They could go back to the Old Farm together. She wouldn't be afraid if Maddy were with her.

Asia had seen a ghost, she was sure of it. It had only been a fleeting glimpse, but she had the distinct impression that the ghost was young and beautiful. Was she the ghost of Miranda Williams, the woman on the auction poster? She picked up another pea pod and slit it open as she tried to decide just how cross Maddy would be.

She sensed Maddy stiffen beside her, and she looked up. Maddy was watching Harry approach the bridge from the other side of the creek.

"He's been talking to his clients," said Asia, wondering why Maddy was staring so hard at Harry. "He does that every night after supper."

Maddy didn't say anything. Her hands lay still in her pea bowl. Asia watched Harry too, all thoughts of the ghost at the Old Farm slipping away. Harry's stride across the bridge and up the slope to the house was purposeful. His face was red.

"Mama." He climbed the steps past Asia and sat down on the edge of the old armchair.

"What is it, Harry?" said Maddy, her voice flat.

Harry leaned forward. His knee jigged up and down. "It seems…ah, it *appears*, that what Sherri told you wasn't true."

Harry didn't exactly call Sherri a liar, but that's what he meant. Asia's heart jumped. Maddy picked up a pea and snapped it open. The peas fell with a soft thump in the bowl. "What wasn't true?" she said finally.

"Sherri said her parents were dead, but she was…well, only her father is dead." Harry paused. "Her mother is alive. Asia's grandmother. I found her."

Maddy's face drained of color. A white noise filled Asia's head. Harry's knee went still and his voice softened. "Her name is Beth Cumfrey. We've just had a long talk. She lives in West Vancouver. That's where Sherri was raised. Not the United States. *West Vancouver.*"

What was Harry talking about? From far away, Asia heard Maddy whisper, "What about Sherri? What did she say about Sherri?"

Harry glanced uneasily at Asia, and Maddy said, "You can talk in front of Asia. We don't keep secrets in this family."

Harry shifted on his chair. "Sherri died, Mama. She was in a car accident in Alberta eight years ago."

Asia's hand froze on a pea pod. She stared at Maddy, frightened. Maddy had turned to stone. Say something, *say* something, Asia willed.

Finally Maddy spoke. "Eight years ago. That's when Sherri left us. Exactly eight years ago." A look of understanding slowly flooded her face.

"Beth said a couple had picked her up hitchhiking. Sherri was the only one who...well, didn't survive. She was riding in the backseat by herself. A transport truck hit them."

Asia felt sick. Did Harry have to say that? What did it matter, anyway? But Maddy was staring hard at Harry. "Did the people who gave her the ride say which way they were going?"

"Yes. They were traveling west. They were almost at the British Columbia border when the accident happened."

"Sherri was coming home," said Maddy. "She was coming home to Cold Creek."

"Actually, we don't know that for—" Maddy gave Harry a penetrating look, and his voice broke off.

A squirrel scrabbled up the trunk of a pine tree, chattering shrilly. Asia watched it numbly. Then Maddy said something that she didn't really understand. "Was this… Beth…terribly angry when you told her that we had Asia?"

"No," said Harry. "She had no idea that Sherri had a daughter." He reached out and took his mother's hand gently. "She was shocked and…*very* excited. But not angry."

~

They told Ira at the hospital the next day.

"Sherri was coming home, Ira," said Maddy. She squeezed his thin papery hand. "She was in Alberta. She was heading for Cold Creek."

Asia couldn't bear the look of bewilderment on Ira's face. She walked over to the window and stared blindly through the glass. She wasn't sure anymore whose side Maddy was on. All that seemed to matter was that Sherri was heading back to British Columbia. Maddy was clinging to that like a drowning person clinging to a life jacket. So maybe her mother hadn't abandoned her after all. Was this supposed to be good news? Did everyone really expect her to *care*? Her shoulders stiffened. She didn't even remember her mother.

"I worked my way through all the Cumfreys in the Vancouver phone book." Harry was retelling his story to Ira. "I found her on the twentieth try…"

Asia turned around and stared helplessly at Ira. He would tell Harry to stop. Her heart ached when she saw a cloud of fear drift across Ira's eyes.

"…she's coming to Cold Creek, Pop. She's driving up the day after tomorrow."

Ira's thin hands quivered on top of the bedspread. "I'll

have to see this Beth person for myself. You'll have to bring her here."

"First, Pop. You'll be the first to see her," said Harry. "I've arranged to meet Beth here at the hospital, and then she can follow us out to Cold Creek."

Ira sank into his pillows.

Maddy said softly, "There was a big brown toad in the garden this morning. The biggest I've seen. It might be a good sign."

Maddy had said that she would never risk losing Asia, would never let anyone take her away. She had told Harry that she and Ira were Asia's family. But Maddy thought the toad in the garden was a good sign. Asia felt her world cave in.

CHAPTER FIFTEEN

"I'm not going," said Asia. "I'm not going to meet her any sooner than I have to."

Harry's face darkened, but she didn't care. She spread peanut butter on a slice of toast and took a big bite. Harry thought she was being rude. He didn't like it when she refused to use Beth Cumfrey's name. He just didn't get it.

"I'm not sure it's up to you," he said. "And besides, you're too young to be left here alone." He pushed his chair back from the table and looked at his watch and frowned. He'd been checking his watch and frowning every few minutes all through breakfast.

"I don't know," said Maddy. She had moved all the canisters onto the end of the table and was scrubbing down the counter. Asia had never seen the kitchen—or the whole house, for that matter—so clean. Maddy had been polishing and dusting ever since she knew that Beth Cumfrey was coming to Cold Creek. "She's twelve. Kids grow up faster in the country. Ira and I left you alone when you were twelve."

Harry looked as if he had forgotten everything about Cold Creek. He was probably an imposter who was after Harry's inheritance. Despite her misery, she grinned, and Harry looked at her coldly. "Your grandmother will think it's strange that you can't be bothered to come and meet her."

Maddy stopped scrubbing and looked worried. This grandmother person hadn't even arrived yet, and already she was having this effect on Maddy. As well as cleaning, Maddy had prepared mountains of food and changed her mind three times about where to put Beth. She finally decided on the spare bedroom, and Harry set up a folding camp cot for himself at the end of the porch.

Asia ignored Harry and pleaded with Maddy. "What I really want to do is go over to Katya's to see the new puppies. And I want to say good-bye—Katya and Anna are going back to Calgary tomorrow."

Maddy slid the bread box away from the wall. "Well, I suppose you'll meet her soon enough. You can take a bag of those plums over to the Hildebrands. But don't forget, you promised to pick flowers for her room."

Maddy called Beth *her* too, thought Asia. Not like Harry. With Harry it was, "Beth said this…Beth said that…," like they were already best friends.

Maddy smiled at Asia. "We'll drop you at Katya's on our way to town."

Relieved, Asia sped outside before Maddy could change her mind. She eyed a big patch of thistles growing beside the woodshed. That's what she wanted to pick—weedy, prickly, ugly, horrible thistles. She hesitated. Maddy wasn't making her go with them, and she better not push her luck. She sighed and headed for the garden.

$\sim$

Katya was bursting with questions. Gert Hildebrand had stopped by to see Maddy yesterday morning and had heard the whole story. "A grandmother you never even heard of! It's so cool," said Katya.

"Not really," said Asia. She sat on the living room floor and cradled a tiny cream puppy in her hands. The mother, Tasha, a pale yellow lab, lay in the middle of an old sheepskin, her eyes weary slits as her puppies scrambled around her.

"What are you going to call her?" said Katya.

"I'm not going to call her anything," said Asia.

Katya looked startled. "You probably have aunts and uncles and maybe cousins too. You'll have to call them something."

Asia hadn't thought about that. It made her want to throw up.

Gert made lunch for the girls, thin slices of brown bread spread with chocolate, which Asia normally loved and was forever begging Maddy to make. Today it tasted like cardboard. She left as soon as they had finished eating, mumbling an excuse about chores. She took a shortcut across the fields and tried not to think about the hurt look on Katya's face. Her stomach tightened. Katya didn't know everything.

She didn't know that Harry was probably going to ask this stranger named Beth to take her away so he could whisk Maddy and Ira off to his precious condominium where everyone hated kids.

He hadn't exactly *said* that, but Asia knew it was true.

CHAPTER SIXTEEN

Asia peered through the thick green branches of her climbing tree. Car tires rumbled on the gravel, and Harry's blue rental car appeared around the bend in the driveway. A bright red sports car followed, slowing and then coming to a stop behind Harry. Car doors banged as Harry and Maddy got out. Asia pulled herself back into the protective branches, her eyes riveted on the red car.

The driver's door opened and a tall slim woman climbed out. She had short gray hair, and she was wearing a denim skirt and a blue striped shirt. She stretched her arms above her head and said something to Maddy. Harry walked over to the car, flipped open the trunk and lifted out a brown suitcase. The woman half-disappeared into the front seat and produced a huge straw beach bag and two plastic grocery sacks. Bits of conversation drifted up to Asia, but it was impossible to make out what anyone was saying. The woman laughed, Maddy smiled and they walked slowly toward the house.

When they got to the porch steps, Harry turned and gestured with his arm. Maddy and the woman stopped and gazed around. Asia's chest tightened. They were looking for her. She stayed as still as she possibly could until finally they disappeared inside. Then she shifted her position on the thick limb and leaned back against the trunk. She could stay in her tree for a very long time. She had done it before.

Half an hour later, Harry opened the door and bellowed her name a few times. He went back inside, and Asia let her breath out slowly. How long could she hide before Maddy started to worry? She wished she had brought her book. Her back was beginning to ache from sitting still for so long when the door opened again, and Maddy walked across the yard. The garden gate squeaked, and then a few minutes later she was back, holding a large red lettuce. Asia stiffened as Maddy hesitated and then walked over to her tree.

"You can stay up there until you're good and ready to come down, Asia Jane Cumfrey." Maddy's voice was clear and calm. "But the rest of us are eating supper in ten minutes, and I won't be keeping a plate warm for you."

There was no fooling Maddy. Asia waited until the porch door clicked shut. Gert's chocolate sandwiches seemed a lifetime ago, and she was starving. Maddy meant what she said. With a huge sigh, she started to climb down.

～

Harry gave her a penetrating look. "Where on earth have you been? Your hair is full of pine needles. And I didn't hear the Hildebrands' car."

Asia didn't say anything. Her eyes flickered uneasily to the woman beside the window. She was standing very still, holding one of Maddy's pots of herbs.

"Asia, this is Beth," said Maddy.

Beth smiled. "Hello, Asia."

"Hello," mumbled Asia. Beth still hadn't moved, and Asia wasn't sure what to do next. But then Maddy lifted a steaming dish out of the oven and said, "Well now, let's everyone sit down," and the embarrassing moment passed.

Asia slid into her place at the big pine table and tried not to look surprised. Maddy had set out the blue flowered china plates from the cabinet in the living room, the dishes that only came out twice a year, at Christmas and Thanksgiving. For a few minutes, no one said anything as the platters of food circled the table. Asia stirred butter into her potatoes and waited for the barrage of questions—what grade are you in, what's your favorite subject, do you like to read?

But Beth turned to Maddy. "Everything looks delicious. Wonderful. And you have an absolutely charming house."

"Well, thank you," said Maddy.

"I was intrigued when Harry said you lived at a place called Cold Creek." Beth helped herself to a mound of carrots and passed the bowl to Maddy. " I thought it had to be a wonderful place. And I can see that it is."

Harry grunted. Maddy looked pleased. "We certainly think so," she said.

Asia chewed on a piece of pork. She had felt so hungry when she came in, but it was hard to swallow. The food stuck like cotton in her throat. Her eyes slid to Beth's plate. She had piled on almost as much food as Harry, and she didn't seem to be having any trouble eating.

Beth laughed. "I'm going to gain ten pounds while I'm here. But everything is wonderful. All these vegetables right out of your garden. I didn't stop for anything on the drive up, and I didn't realize how hungry I was."

Asia tried to count how many times Beth had said the word wonderful. Every time, Maddy looked pleased. It didn't mean anything. Couldn't Maddy see that? She sighed and let the conversation float around her. At least they weren't forcing her to talk. She tuned in and out, only half listening until they discussed Ira.

"I thought he looked wonderful," said Beth, "considering everything."

Considering what? thought Asia. And how would you know? No one seemed to be in a hurry to finish eating. Maddy had been up late last night making a huge iced coconut cake that gleamed like a snowy mountain. The meal was going to take forever.

Harry was interested in Beth's sports car. "I bought it last year," said Beth. She moved her fork around in the air when she talked, and three silver bracelets jangled on her wrist. Three! thought Asia. "My daughter Valerie talked me into it. After Ward died, she said I should get something that wasn't for old ladies. Ward always bought Volvos."

"Ward?" said Maddy gently.

"I'm sorry. Ward was my husband. He died two years ago from a stroke."

"Asia's grandfather," said Harry.

That was obvious. Heat flooded Asia's cheeks.

"Anyway," said Beth smoothly, "my granddaughter Sierra loves it. She's eight, and she thinks it's very cool."

You'll have aunts and uncles and cousins and everything, Katya had said. Asia pushed away her plate. She couldn't force down one more bite.

Maddy had stopped eating too, but she seemed fascinated by everything Beth was saying. "Sierra is a pretty name. How many grandchildren do you have?"

Did Asia imagine it, or did Beth hesitate just for a second? "Three. Sierra, her brother Ben, who's five, and Asia."

They were talking about her as if she were invisible. And why didn't anyone ask the real question, the question that had been screaming silently at them all through supper. Why didn't they ask Beth why Sherri said she had no family? Why she said her parents were dead?

Maddy poured coffee and suggested they sit for a few minutes before having cake. Now was a good time to leave. The thought of coconut cake made Asia feel sick.

Harry was in the middle of a very boring and seemingly endless story about a fort he built when he was a boy, and she waited for a break to excuse herself. Beth must be regretting asking Harry if things had changed much since he grew up at Cold Creek, Asia thought with some satisfaction. She snuck a look at her face. She was watching Harry intently, but her mouth had a squeezed look as if she was holding back a smile. Her eyes flickered across the table to Asia. She winked.

"Can I be excused?" Asia blurted out. When Maddy nodded, she pushed back her chair and escaped outside. She stood on the porch and took a big steadying breath. Her grandmother's wink had caught her by surprise. She liked it better when everyone was ignoring her.

CHAPTER SEVENTEEN

Miranda stood in the doorway of her house and scanned the hillside. She twisted her hands together. Something must have happened to keep the people away. She had seen no one for three days—not since the night they had come to the Old Farm. The night she had scared Asia so badly.

She adjusted her bonnet, shut the door carefully behind her and set off up the hill to the new house. Her apprehension grew when she passed the dog's grave with the pale wooden cross. The flowers on the grave had wilted and died. What could have happened to make everyone forget about the old dog?

Miranda faltered when she got to the log bridge. She didn't have the courage to step foot on it today. But she could see enough from where she was standing. Two strange cars were parked beside the house, one blue, and one small and bright red and unlike anything she had ever seen at Cold Creek. She spotted Maddy in her rocking chair on the porch, her head nodded forward as if she were asleep. She couldn't remember ever seeing Maddy sleep in the middle of the afternoon. Her arthritis must be acting up, she thought with a pang of sympathy.

The screen door opened, and a tall gray-haired woman she had never seen before came out, carrying a tray with a teapot and mugs. The woman said something and set the tray down on a small table. Maddy sat up and the woman poured the tea. Then she settled into the old armchair beside Maddy.

The two women looked as if they were comfortable with each other. They were enjoying the tea in a compan-ionable way. Miranda's own loneliness welled up inside her. She waited to see if Asia would appear, but she didn't. Finally she turned and started on the long walk back to the Old Farm. She understood now why Maddy and Asia's routine had changed, why she hadn't seen them for days. It was because of the stranger, the tall woman with the gray hair.

~

It was a hot afternoon without a breath of wind, but the long grass ahead of Miranda rippled. "Montgomery, is that you?" she called. "Come out, you bad boy. Come out and I'll carry you home."

She waited for the answering meow, for her cat to spring out of the grass and wrap himself around her legs, but everything was silent. She frowned. A coyote had been hanging around. She had spotted it several times, but she didn't think this was a coyote.

Her chest felt queer, as if it were tightening around her heart. She walked faster and then broke into a run, following the swaying grass. She saw a flash of blue, a hair ribbon in the sun. Miranda's head suddenly ached, and her thoughts spun out of control. She stumbled through the grass. She had a glimpse of a blue pinafore, sun shining on glossy brown hair. "Daisy, wait! Don't run away!" she cried.

The grass swirled. Tiny boots pounded on the hard dry ground.

"Stop, Daisy! Stop!"

The grass parted. The tiny elf-like girl peering at her through the yellow green stalks was Beatrice, not Daisy. Beatrice's small body was shaking with ragged sobs. Tears streaked down her scarlet cheeks, leaving two smudgy trails. "Papa! Where is my Papa?" she cried.

Miranda tried to speak, but her face was frozen and her lips wouldn't move. She reached for Beatrice, but the little girl had vanished. Miranda was alone again, the meadow a motionless sea of golden grass. She sank onto her knees and tried to pull her frantic thoughts together. It must be the strain of the last few days, she thought wildly. Her mind was playing tricks.

After a long time, she stood up and continued across the meadow. When she reached the Old Farm, the scent of something sweet floated through the air. It was the lavender that grew almost wild in her garden beside the porch. She stooped down and picked a few purple stalks. She pressed them to her face, trying to steady her nerves.

Then she crumpled them and dropped them into the grass. "Papa! Where is my Papa!" Beatrice had cried.

Miranda's head pounded. She wiped her eyes. She had to get inside her house, right away. The smell of lavender was sickening.

June 22, 1915

George has business to attend to in town, and Beatrice and I have accompanied him for a treat. We are staying one night in the hotel, and then we will go home because surely tomorrow Ridley Blackmore will be back!

We expected Blackmore a week ago. It has been raining for days, heavy spring rains, and George says that it might be the rain that is delaying the man. In a rash moment, I told George that I hoped Blackmore would never come back. He didn't say anything, but he looked quite shocked.

A woman approached our table in the dining room at the hotel. It was Mabel Anderson, a widow who has been staying with her son in Vancouver for two years. It all happened so quickly and I had no time to think. I shall write exactly what she said.

"Miranda! George! How wonderful to see you. And is this poppet really your dear Daisy? How old is she now?"

I heard myself reply, "She is four years old. Our Daisy is small for her age."

Beatrice paid no attention. I had allowed her to bring her doll to the table and she was playing with it in her lap. The silly woman's eyes lingered on her, and a small frown played on her forehead. George sat in smoldering silence, his face purple. When the woman finally sailed to the next table, he accused me of lying to myself and to our friends.

Beatrice watched us with puzzled eyes. I wiped the little girl's creamy chin with a napkin. My heart was racing. I informed George tartly that Mabel Anderson was hardly a friend and that it had done no harm. Later, I tucked Beatrice into the tall four-poster bed in our room. She was crying because George was so angry. She fell asleep clutching her doll, from which she has become inseparable.

I am sitting at the window writing this. A man in town developed the photograph of Beatrice, and I have propped it against the oil lamp on the table. The little girl looks solemnly out at me from the picture, her hand resting on Montgomery's back.

The shutters are closed, but loud voices from the muddy street below are drifting up through the window. The men are having a contest to see whose pair of horses can pull the heaviest load. George is out there somewhere, still sulking over my behavior. Before stomping outside to join the men, he vowed to tell Blackmore when he returns that he and Beatrice must leave Cold Creek.

George doesn't understand. God took my beautiful Daisy away from me. I will never let anyone take Beatrice.

CHAPTER EIGHTEEN

"I like Beth," said Maddy.

Asia's heart jumped. She concentrated on peeling a strip of loose wood off the edge of the porch step. "But you like Harry too," she muttered finally.

Maddy threw back her head and laughed. Asia hadn't heard her laugh like that since before Ira got sick. "And that makes you wonder about my judgment."

Asia shrugged. Maddy rested her knitting in her lap and massaged her fingers gently. "Of course I like Harry." Her eyes twinkled. "He's my son. And he came right away. We need him here. How would we get back and forth from the hospital, for one thing?"

"I could drive us," said Asia. Maddy smiled, and Asia couldn't hold back a faint smile too. And then her misery flooded over her. "Everything is changing because of Harry," she said. She abandoned the piece of wood and squeezed her hands between her knees.

Maddy was quiet for a few minutes. "I always knew there must be someone like Beth out there," she said at last. "A grandparent, an aunt, an uncle. It only made sense. At first, Ira wanted to look. But I was afraid."

Asia hadn't known that about Ira. Maddy said there were no secrets in this family, but it wasn't true. She felt sick when she thought about all the things no one ever told her.

"Ira loves you to pieces," said Maddy. "We both do. And we'll always be your family. But we should have tried to find your other family. Harry is right."

Maddy was speaking carefully, but Asia couldn't control her anger any longer. "Harry should have minded his own business! He should have left us alone!"

Maddy looked sad. Asia's eyes burned. She stared hard at her knees. She had one last thing to say. "If Beth is so great, then why did my mother say she was dead?"

Part of her wanted to shock Maddy. But Maddy was unshockable. "I've thought and thought about that too," she admitted. "When Harry told us he'd found her, I thought she must be some kind of monster. But as soon as I met her, I realized there are two sides to this story. And now it just doesn't seem to matter."

It did matter. Asia dug her fingernails into the palms of her hands. How could Maddy say that?

"The important thing right now is to get Ira better," said Maddy. "And then we'll sort all this out."

Is that what Maddy thought they were doing, sorting things out? The tears escaped from Asia's eyes and flooded her cheeks. She pushed away Maddy's quick touch on her arm and jumped off the porch and ran.

~

Asia opened the door of Ira's workshop and slipped into the cool building. The smell of wood shavings and varnish lingered in every corner. It was easy to pretend that Ira had just stepped out. That the heart attack hadn't happened.

Asia walked beside the shelves, lightly tracing her fingers over the boxes. The gleaming eyes of bears and rabbits and birds glinted in the sunlight from the windows. She could hear Ira's soft voice. "Now that's a mischievous look on that squirrel. What do you think of putting a snowshoe rabbit on the new pine box?"

Footsteps crunched on the gravel outside. Asia froze.

Beth's head popped through the doorway. "I've been exploring. I just discovered Maddy's garden. What a wonderful place to escape from the world. I don't think I've ever been anywhere as peaceful."

Asia felt exactly the same way when she was in Maddy's garden. But she was silent. If this was an invitation to talk, she wasn't taking the bait.

Beth stepped inside. She was wearing a floppy sunhat today, and her long bare arms jangled with bracelets. "Ira told me about his boxes when we were at the hospital. Do you mind if I have a look?"

Asia hid her surprise and shrugged. Somehow she hadn't imagined Beth and Ira talking. She had pictured Ira lying on his pillows, his face gray with disapproval, while Beth rattled on about how wonderful everything was. What else had Ira said to her?

"I understand you know the secret to every box," said Beth. "Ira says you're a huge help to him." She picked up a smooth round box with a swallow on the lid. "This is lovely. Don't tell me. Let me see if I can figure it out myself."

Asia watched her for a few minutes as she turned the box sideways and upside down. "I give up," she said finally, with one eyebrow raised.

Asia walked over and took the box from Beth. "It's this wing," she said. "You have to move it just the right way."

She pressed one of the swallow's wings, and a tiny drawer slid out of the lid of the box.

"Ingenious!" said Beth. "A perfect hiding place." She glanced along the shelves filled with gleaming boxes. "What a treasure trove. I told Ira I'd love a box, and he recommended letting you choose for me."

Asia knew which one she would pick for herself. It was one of the smallest boxes, tucked at the end of the bottom shelf. The smooth curved sides were made of red cherry, and the oval lid was inlaid with a wolf howling at a sliver of moon. The moon was the key to the secret compartment. Tourists overlooked the little box when they came to Cold Creek, and Asia secretly prayed that it would never sell.

"Maybe one of the whale boxes," she muttered, steering Beth away from the wolf box. "Lots of people like the whale boxes." She reached up to the top shelf and lifted down a big square box with a killer whale arching across the lid. She showed Beth how to press one of the whale's flukes and slide out the secret drawer.

"Perfect," said Beth. "I live near the ocean, so it will have special meaning."

Asia tightened inside. Now she was supposed to ask Beth about her house in West Vancouver. Pretend to be interested. This whole thing was probably just an excuse for the let's-get-to-know-my-granddaughter talk.

"These boxes are valuable," said Asia loudly. "You better tell Maddy you're taking one of them." She paused. "So you can pay her."

Beth's gray eyes looked at Asia evenly. "Of course. I'll take it over to the house and talk to her about it right now."

Her grandmother had got the point. So why did Asia feel worse instead of better? After Beth left, she stayed behind in the quiet workshop. She tried to recapture the feeling of Ira, but he had disappeared. She brushed a pile of sawdust off his workbench and watched Beth through the wide side window, talking to Harry beside the house, showing him the box. Harry was smiling.

Everybody likes her, thought Asia. Maddy, Harry and maybe even Ira. Everybody but her.

CHAPTER NINETEEN

Ira had been moved back into Intensive Care for one day. It wasn't another heart attack, the doctors said quickly, but clearly Ira had given them a scare. Within twenty-four hours he had stabilized again and was back in his old room. He might be ready to be moved by the end of next week, the doctors said cautiously.

Harry made more phone calls to California and cancelled more appointments. Maddy talked to Joyce, Harry's wife, for almost an hour.

That night, Asia heard the murmuring voices of Beth and Maddy and Harry in the living room as she lay on her bed upstairs, pretending to read. She thought they would never stop talking. Finally, Maddy came upstairs and sat on the bed and explained everything to her.

By the time Maddy had finished talking, a hard knot had filled Asia's throat. "I hate Harry. And I hate Beth."

"No," said Maddy.

Asia focused on a spray of wallpaper roses. She kept her eyes rigidly open, forcing the tears back. "Why are you making me go with her?" she whispered.

"Because it's the very best thing I can think of to do," said Maddy simply.

Asia picked up her book and stared stonily at the page until Maddy left.

~

"Asia's not going anywhere on a Friday," said Maddy. "Fridays are not safe for traveling. It's completely out of the question."

"How about Saturday?" said Harry. "It would be a good idea to get her down there so she has time to settle in before school starts."

School. Asia froze outside the kitchen door. Maddy was silent. "Then that's settled," said Harry.

"That only gives Asia two days to get ready," said Beth. "Is that enough time?"

Two days. A lifetime and no time at all.

Bacon sizzled in a frying pan. Cutlery rattled. Asia knew she would throw up if she ate anything. She turned around and slipped out the back door.

~

Harry generated a series of lists on his laptop and taped them in strategic places in the house—lists with headings like *Take to California, Put in Storage, Throw Away, Neighbors Who Might Take Livestock, Ira's Boxes—Send Mail Orders? Gift Shop?*

Maddy picked armfuls of vegetables from the garden—
purple beets, huge lettuces, leafy stalks of Swiss chard and
golden zucchini—and packed them in a box to fit in the
trunk of Beth's car. Cartons sprang up everywhere, slowly
filling with clothes, books, shoes. By noon the heat was sti-
fling, and Maddy made everyone take an iced tea break on
the porch. Asia took hers to her room. She leaned over her
windowsill and watched the gray clouds building over the
mountains.

In the afternoon, Harry drove Maddy and Asia to the
hospital. Maddy slipped a newspaper-wrapped bundle into
Ira's arms, and then she and Harry went to the cafeteria
to give Asia and Ira some time alone. Ira presented the
package solemnly to Asia. Her heart thudding, she tore the
newspaper off in strips, making a sea of shredded paper on
Ira's bed. It was the cherry box with the wolf on the lid.

Asia started to cry, and Ira said, "Beth tells me you can
see the Pacific Ocean right from her house if you stand on
the roof!" Asia stopped crying and laughed.

"It's the same ocean all the dang way to California," said
Ira. "Imagine that. You and Maddy and I will be looking at the
same ocean. We'll send messages back and forth in bottles."

Asia read Ira all his get-well cards. She told him about
Tasha's puppies. Too soon, Harry's voice sounded in the
hall. He had come to pick her up. Panic rose in her chest.

Ira heard too. He leaned closer to her. "Now you
remember, we're just migrating for the winter." He
squeezed her hand. "And d'you know what's special about
migrating birds?"

Asia shook her head. The tears were pooling behind her eyes again.

"They always come back," said Ira.

～

The rain started in the late afternoon, big spattery drops on the windows that quickly became a downpour and then settled into a persistent drizzle by the time they had finished eating supper. Maddy sent Asia upstairs to finish packing. She stood still for a minute, looking at the two worn stuffed rabbits on the pillow at the top of her bed. She called them Boy Rabbit and Lucky Rabbit, and they had slept beside her for as long as she could remember. Their dark button eyes looked anxious and she whispered, "Don't worry. You're coming too."

She wrapped Ira's wolf box in a sweatshirt and tucked it in the corner of her duffel bag. Then she crammed in some shirts and socks. She flopped down on her bed. She made a list in her head of all the things she wanted to take with her but couldn't. Her bicycle, a chicken, Maddy's sheep, the creek, her climbing tree.

She tiptoed downstairs. The house was quiet. Beth was in the living room, reading in the armchair by the window, and Harry and Maddy had disappeared. Asia grabbed her jacket and slipped outside. She stood on the porch for a few minutes, deciding what to do. The rain had stopped, and Maddy was by the garden fence, in her yellow slicker and hat, trying to prop up the last of the delphiniums. She was struggling with twine and stakes. What was the point? Why didn't she just let them collapse? Everybody would be gone soon anyway.

Asia set off across the bridge. She trudged across the dripping meadow as far as Dandy's grave. With everything that had happened, she had neglected it. She whispered an apology to Dandy, and then picked fresh flowers and threw the old ones over the creek bank. She glanced in the direction of the Old Farm. She had never told Maddy about the ghost, and now she wondered if she had imagined the whole thing. There was no feeling today of being watched, unless you counted the small brown squirrel who chattered at her from the shelter of a fir tree.

She walked home along the creek, stepping carefully over the wet slippery rocks. Just before she got to the bridge, she spotted someone standing on a big flat boulder, tossing stones into the water. Asia stiffened. Ira! she thought. Then the person looked up and said, "Oh, hi, Asia." It was Harry, in Ira's old plaid coat and a floppy hat.

It was impossible to pretend she hadn't seen him. "Hi," she mumbled.

"I was just thinking about Terror," said Harry. "He was an old black lab we got from the SPCA. He used to come down to the creek every day and dive for rocks. He'd plunge in, right underwater, and pick up a rock and bring it up on the bank. By the end of the summer, he'd have made a big pile on the shore. It sounds impossible, but he did."

Asia could picture it easily. The wet dog, looking like a sleek black otter in the water. Dandy had loved the water too, but just to splash in on hot days. She was staring at Harry and realized he might think she was interested. She turned to leave.

"Hello!" cried Maddy. She stood on the other side of the creek, bright in her yellow slicker, smiling at them. "What are you two doing down there?"

"I was telling Asia about Terror," Harry called back. "Come and join us!"

Maddy walked across the bridge and down over the rocks. "Asia, help me settle on this log."

Asia eased Maddy onto the log. Maddy gave a small wince, which she dismissed with a wave of her hand.

"Do you remember Terror?" said Harry.

"I do indeed," said Maddy. "He was a good dog. We've had a lot of good dogs at Cold Creek."

For a second, Asia felt the touch of Dandy's cold nose on her hand. Somewhere in the grass near the bridge, a frog burst into song. She took a slow deep breath. She wondered if it were possible to absorb all the smells of Cold Creek at once: the pine trees, the wet grass, the faint scent of wild mint.

She tilted her face to the sky. It was drizzling again, and the misty rain sprinkled her cheeks with tiny pinpricks. The unfamiliar weight of something smooth and cold bumped against her neck. The silver medal that Maddy had given her last night, just before she went to bed. "It's Saint Christopher, the patron saint of travelers," Maddy had explained. Asia had pretended not to care, burying her face in her pillow until Maddy left her room.

When Maddy was safely downstairs, Asia had taken it out of its little box and examined it. She understood right away that the medal hanging from the delicate chain was powerful. It was a silver oval with an engraving in the center of a man wading across a river. The man carried a staff in one hand and a little child on his shoulders. Around the edges of the medal were the words *Saint Christopher Protect Us.* Asia liked feeling it on her neck. She vowed that she would never take it off.

Harry tossed a stone in the water. "I'm going to bring Joyce here one day," he said. "She's never seen Cold Creek."

"Next summer," said Maddy. "We'll bring her next summer."

She folded her hands neatly together. Rain dripped from the rim of her hat into her lap. "Next summer I think we'll try turkeys. And I want Ira to build that greenhouse he's promised me for so long. And Asia, you might want to think about trying to raise your own sheep."

Asia didn't say anything. Her anger at Maddy had slipped away somewhere for awhile, but that was not the same as forgiving her.

Next summer.

Maddy had promised that Saint Christopher would keep her safe.

All she had to do was hold on until next summer.

June 18, 1915

My head has ached all day. George is still determined to tell Ridley Blackmore that he and Beatrice must leave Cold Creek. He spent most of the day searching for the man. When he sat down for his meal, he reported gloomily that he had seen no sign of him.

George had to ride all the way to the Warners' bridge to cross the creek because our bridge is washing out and is not safe. The Warners' homestead is seven miles downstream. He was exhausted, and he ate his meal in silence. Later he told me that he has put a log across our bridge to warn Blackmore not to cross. He said that the bottom timbers are gone and that a man alone might be able to walk across it, but it will never take the weight of horses.

Beatrice is fretting tonight. It is late, but she cries if I put her to bed. I have finally given up and allowed her to stay with us. The rain sounds like pebbles hitting the windows and is making my head much worse.

CHAPTER TWENTY

Montgomery lay in Miranda's lap and purred while she stroked his ears. The promise of rain was in the air and in the rustling aspen leaves outside the window. They needed it. Her flowers were withering and the grass was bone dry. Miranda's hands stilled and her eyes drifted shut. Just a short nap, and then she would go outside and finish tending Daisy's grave before the rain started.

Miranda dreamed of fresh ocean breezes and waves lapping the shore. She dreamed of seagulls squabbling on the rocks and cormorants drying their huge black wings in the sun. Montgomery studied his mistress's face, and then jumped with a soft thud to the floor. He stalked across the room, tail flicking, and leaped up on the table by the window, his claws skidding on the lace cloth. He stared out the window at the leaves blowing on the trees and the heavy rolling gray clouds.

The first drops of rain spattered against the glass. Miranda stirred in her chair. She stood up stiffly and walked over to the window. She rested her hand on Montgomery's back and watched the dark skies open.

It had rained hard in the spring of 1915, their last spring at Cold Creek. Gray day after gray day, Beatrice's face pressed against the streaming glass, until the wagon road was a sea of mud and the usually mild creek a raging river. "Do you remember the rain, Montgomery?" she said softly. "You hated it, you and Beatrice."

Montgomery leaped onto the floor, the fur along his spine ruffled. Miranda slid back the bolt on the door, and they stepped outside into the dark wet night.

〜

Something woke Asia in the night.

A soft thump.

She lay very still. Her eyes slowly focused in the dark and slid over the familiar gray shapes—the night table, the dresser, the mirror on the wall. And two new shapes: the duffel bag and the suitcase by the door.

Another thump. It was coming from her windowsill.

She slid out of bed and crossed the room, her bare feet making no noise on the wooden floor. She pressed her face against the cold glass.

Two amber slits stared back at her. A mouth opened in a silent yawn, showing a row of sharp teeth. The cat! Asia slid the window up and called, "Here, kitty! Here, kitty!"

The cat leaped from the sill to the branch of an tree. It huddled in a gray ball, its amber eyes glowing

Asia leaned out the window. Water dripped from the leaves of the tree, and the air felt sodden, but it had finally stopped raining. Tattered black clouds raced across the sky, and a full round moon cast a pale watery light over the creek.

Asia stiffened. Someone was on the bridge…a shadowy gray figure, tall and willowy, staring at the water. She frowned. Was it Beth? What was she doing on the bridge in the middle of the night? She watched the figure turn and gaze up at the house. It was the ghost from the Old Farm. This time she had a clear image of her—the long blue dress, a pale beautiful face, wild flowing hair.

"Miranda?" shouted Asia. "Are you Miranda Williams?"

The ghost cried out, a long tormented wail that sent prickles up and down Asia's spine. It was the saddest sound she had ever heard. Then clouds scudded over the moon, and the ghost faded into a gray shadow. She floated across the bridge and vanished into the meadow.

Shivering, Asia searched the tree for the cat, but it was gone.

She crept back to bed.

She was freezing.

CHAPTER TWENTY-ONE

Miranda stood in the trees beside the sheep barn. The bright red car slowed at the bend in the driveway. A horn honked. Maddy and the man stood arm in arm in front of the house and waved. Miranda glimpsed a white face framed with black hair staring through the back window. And then the car was gone.

Asia wasn't coming back for a long time. Miranda knew that. She had watched the man load the suitcases and bags, the vegetables and flowers, into the trunk and backseat of the car. She ached with exhaustion. She had wandered all night, in the meadows and beside the creek. Her punishment had become unbearable, this eternal prison on earth, trapped by the dark secret of her life, while she yearned to escape to the world of the dead.

Her head bowed as she walked across the meadow to the Old Farm. Asia was the only one who had ever heard her speak, and she was gone. Miranda would leave too, and return to her other place. There was nothing to keep her at Cold Creek any longer.

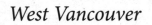

West Vancouver

CHAPTER TWENTY-TWO

Beth lived in a tall brown house on the side of a steep hill, halfway between the ocean and the mountains. She took Asia to a little bedroom on the second floor. "You can put your things in here. This was Sherri's room. Your mother loved the view of the mountains from here, so I thought it would be a good choice for you."

Beth sounded so casual when she said Sherri's name. Asia dumped her duffel bag on the floor and looked around. The wallpaper was pale yellow stripes and there was a dresser and a night table, both painted yellow. "Yellow was Sherri's favorite color," said Beth, and just for a second her voice sounded different. Asia didn't say anything. She stood beside her bag while Beth walked over to the window and slid it open. A faint scent of evergreen trees and flowers drifted into the room.

"I'll take you on a quick tour of the rest of the house, and then you'll probably want to unpack." Beth's voice was brisk now. "There's space in the cupboard for you, and the dresser is empty."

Asia trailed downstairs behind Beth. Thick cream carpets muffled their footsteps. There were windows everywhere, even some in the ceiling, which Beth called skylights. Asia counted three other bedrooms and two bathrooms. Next to Beth's bedroom was a tiny cluttered room with a computer, bookshelves and a table buried in papers. "This is where I work," said Beth. "I'm a writer."

Asia had heard Beth and Maddy talking about Beth's work, but she hadn't paid much attention. Now she felt a flicker of interest. "You mean like an author?"

"That's right." Beth smiled. "Non-fiction only. I write mostly articles for magazines, and I'm researching a book."

"Oh." It sounded very boring. If Asia had a room like this, she would write mystery novels. She turned away, and they continued the tour in silence, through a big sunny kitchen with pots of geraniums in the windows and kids' drawings stuck on the fridge. There were three rooms just for sitting and reading or watching TV—the living room, a sunroom and the den.

The den was the only room Asia liked. The chairs in it looked old, crowded bookshelves climbed all the way to the ceiling, and there was a TV. The den looked like it belonged in the house at Cold Creek.

"This is my favorite room," said Beth, as if she had read

Asia's mind. "Since Ward died, I spend most of my time in here. I confess I've even got in the habit of eating supper in front of the TV."

Asia didn't answer her. She stared at a collection of framed photographs on the wall. Strangers' faces stared back at her. A woman in a foamy white wedding dress holding hands with a man in a black suit. Beth and a tall man with a dark mustache, leaning against the railing of a ship. A freckle-faced girl with pigtails. A little blond boy missing his two front teeth. A teenage girl with long black hair, looking sideways out of the picture and laughing. Asia's heart started to hammer.

"Maddy said you've never seen a picture of your mother," said Beth softly. "I should have thought to bring some photo albums up to Cold Creek with me. Everything just happened so fast. That one was taken the summer Sherri turned fifteen."

Asia swallowed. She couldn't pull her eyes away from the photograph of the girl with the black hair. Her mother had been very pretty. She had a slim face and an upturned nose. Asia had always thought that her own face was too round and her nose too straight. But their hair was the same.

"It gave me a start when I first saw you," said Beth. "You're so alike. Sherri used to tell people she was half native and that we adopted her. But actually your hair comes from Ward's side of the family. Your great-grandmother had long black hair right to her waist and she never cut it, even when it turned snow white."

"Oh," said Asia.

"This is my other daughter, Valerie, and her husband, Sam, on their wedding day. And that's Sierra, of course, and Ben. Those are their latest school pictures. And that handsome man with me is your grandfather."

The air in the room felt hot and close. Asia put her hand on the back of an armchair to steady herself. "It's a lot to take in all at once." Beth sounded far away. "Look, why don't you go upstairs and get yourself settled in? I'll make something simple for supper, and we'll be couch potatoes tonight."

Asia had never been in a house as big as Beth's. She wandered into the two bathrooms before she found her bedroom again. She unpacked quickly, her mind blank as she found places to put her things: shirts and jeans in the dresser drawers, runners and sandals against the wall, Lucky Rabbit and Boy Rabbit on the night table beside the bed. She opened the cupboard door hesitantly, but it was empty except for a dozen coat hangers and some cardboard boxes pushed to the back. This had been her mother's room, but she couldn't see one single thing that might have belonged to her.

She unpacked Ira's wolf box last. She set it on the night table beside the rabbits and ran her fingers over the smooth wood. She pressed the moon and slid open the secret drawer. She had put two of her best lucky charms in the drawer—a four-leaf clover that she had pressed between books and a smooth creek stone with a hole worn in the middle. She sighed and closed the drawer. Her charms weren't working anymore.

She put the box down, walked over to the window and leaned on the sill. *Your mother loved the view of the mountains from here.* Asia frowned and looked away from the hazy mountains into the backyard, where an emerald green lawn was shaded by large evergreen trees. There were neighbors on either side, their houses and yards partly hidden by high wooden fences, though she caught a glimpse of a turquoise swimming pool behind the house on the right.

Asia's eyes flickered to a huge tree in the back corner of Beth's yard. She studied it. She wasn't sure what kind it was. It was a giant of a tree, towering above the fence, its long curving limbs covered with broad silver-green leaves. One long branch swept low to the ground. For a second, the heaviness in her chest shifted slightly. She leaned farther out the window. It just might make a good climbing tree.

~

Beth gave Asia a quick lesson on operating the DVD player, and Asia picked out a movie from the supply of DVDs in the little cupboard under the TV. During supper, Beth seemed tired, and Asia was thankful that watching a movie meant they didn't have to talk. She went upstairs to have a shower and was standing beside her bed, combing out her wet hair, when Beth tapped on the door.

"Come in," said Asia.

"Maddy phoned while you were in the shower," said Beth from the doorway. "It was a bit of a funny connection, but everything is fine there."

Asia's throat thickened. "It's a radiophone," she muttered. "It always sounds like that."

She glanced at her grandmother and then looked away quickly. Beth was holding a brown paper bag. It was probably a present, which she would have to pretend to like.

"Did you want to call Maddy back?"

"I'll call her tomorrow."

There was a pause. Asia's stomach churned. Beth didn't understand that she couldn't talk to Maddy right now. Maddy had sided with Harry and Beth, and Asia was never going to forgive her.

Beth said, "Well then, I'll leave you to get to bed. But I wanted you to have this first."

She walked across the room and handed the bag to Asia. The brown paper was creased and limp. There was something soft and squishy inside. Whatever it was, she would pretend to be pleased, and then maybe Beth would leave her alone.

She opened the bag and lifted out a stuffed rabbit made of soft pale-blue fur. It had black button eyes and long floppy ears lined with pink satin.

"It was in Sherri's suitcase," said Beth. "After the accident, the police returned her belongings to us. She had just bought it. The receipt was still in the bag."

Asia's heart thudded. Her throat felt dry.

"I had no idea who it was for. But I just couldn't bring myself to give it away." Beth's eyes flickered to the two limp well-loved rabbits propped up on the night table. "There's no doubt now that she bought it for you."

Asia couldn't trust herself to speak, but Beth didn't seem to notice. "You're exhausted, and we have lots of time tomorrow to talk. Do you want to borrow a hair dryer or are you going to crawl in with wet hair?"

Asia swallowed. "Wet hair."

She waited until Beth had shut the door and then sank onto the bed. Beth was right, every bone in her body ached with tiredness. She propped the blue rabbit on the night table, between Lucky Rabbit and Boy Rabbit, turned out the light and slid under the sheet.

When Harry had told Maddy and Asia about the car accident, Maddy had said right away, "Sherri was coming home, she was coming home to Cold Creek." Maddy hadn't needed proof. But she would like to know about the rabbit. Asia rolled over on her side and gazed at the rabbit's bright black eyes. For a second, they seemed to gaze back at her with a mixture of sadness and wisdom.

"You need a name," she said. A wave of sleepiness washed over her. In the distance she heard the phone ring and Beth's footsteps on the stairs. "Lost Rabbit," she whispered. "I'm going to call you Lost Rabbit."

CHAPTER TWENTY-THREE

In the morning, Beth took Asia to the bike store and let her pick out a brand-new bike. "I bought one for Sierra last month for her eighth birthday, and she's dying for someone to ride with," she said. "Besides, with a bicycle, you won't have to depend on me to get around."

Asia had heard Beth on the phone that morning talking to someone about deadlines. It had something to do with the book she was researching. Her grandmother had sounded terribly busy. Underneath her friendly manner she probably secretly regarded Asia as a huge inconvenience.

But Beth didn't seem to be in a big hurry this morning. They brought the bike home on a carrier on the back of the car, and Beth helped Asia adjust the seat and showed her how to work the gears. Then, with a regretful, "The book is calling me," she left Asia alone to practice in the driveway and on the street in front of the house. Asia had never ridden on pavement before, and she loved the way her tires whirred on the smooth surface. At lunch, an idea formed in her mind, and she pushed her sandwich around her plate, trying to gather her courage to ask. She was twelve years old, and she didn't want to be treated like a little kid. Besides, Beth had bought her the bike so she could be more independent.

"I think I'll go to the library." Beth had pointed it out to her on their way here, and Asia was pretty sure she could find her way around. But her voice came out louder than she had intended. Beth paused in the middle of pouring tea and Asia muttered, "Is that okay?"

"You don't think it's too soon to go out on your own?" said Beth.

"No, I don't," said Asia. "Maddy says kids grow up faster in the country."

A smile flickered across Beth's face, and Asia frowned. It wasn't supposed to be funny.

Beth stirred sugar into her tea. "Well, in that case, as long as you wear your helmet and watch out for the traffic, I don't see why not." She smiled broadly this time, but Asia pretended not to notice and concentrated on her sandwich.

～

Maddy phoned again, just as she was leaving. She heard Beth say, "I'll try to catch her," and she slipped out the front door.

The first part was easy, straight down the steep hill almost to the ocean. Asia braked at the stop signs and kept her eyes peeled for cars. The traffic was much heavier when she reached Marine Drive. She stopped for a minute to catch her breath, frightened by the steady stream of cars. Then she remembered her Saint Christopher medal, bumping against her neck. Saint Christopher, the patron saint of travelers. He probably kept a special eye out for people on bikes.

She rode along the street of shops and kept going until she spotted the stone building that was the library. She chained her bike to a rack and went inside. The library at home was just one room, and it was hard to find something she hadn't already read. Here there were rooms and rooms of books, and there was even an elevator to take you to more rooms.

The children's section was empty, except for a woman at a desk tapping busily on a computer, and a teenage girl reading a story to a group of toddlers in the corner. Most kids probably had better things to do on a hot summer afternoon, but Asia didn't care. She settled herself in a corner with three enticing mysteries and was soon lost in a story about four friends exploring an abandoned mine.

She was surprised when she glanced up at the clock to see that a whole hour had passed. The toddlers were picking out picturebooks to take home, and the woman at the computer had disappeared. She wondered uneasily if it was safe to have left her bike unattended for so long. She stood up and stretched and then took her mysteries downstairs to the front desk. Beth had given her a note so she could get her own card, and she waited while a librarian typed in her information.

The librarian slid the books across the counter with a smile. "Back to school soon."

Asia didn't say anything. School was a huge black cloud looming in the distance. So far Beth hadn't mentioned it, and Asia prayed desperately that she would forget until it was too late. Did schools fill up? Was there even a tiny *tiny* chance that someone would tell them, "I'm sorry, we've got no more room, please come back next year."

"Enjoy the rest of your summer," said the librarian. Asia slid the books into her backpack and went outside. To her relief, her bike was still there. She rode back along Marine Drive, watching carefully for red lights and turning cars. The traffic was scary but she was already getting the hang of it. If Maddy and Ira could see her now!

Maddy. Asia tensed and concentrated on the next busy intersection. It was easy really. In no time she was back in front of the big grocery store at the corner where you turned to go up the hill to Beth's house. She rested her foot on the pavement and watched a family with three young kids walk across the street, eating ice-cream cones and carrying sand toys. It was boiling hot and the climb up the long hill would be horrible.

She thought about Beth's big silent house with the closed-in yard. Beth was probably working on her deadlines, relieved that Asia was out of the way. She made up her mind quickly. She hopped back on her bike and headed toward the ocean. Nobody cared where she was. She could ride her brand-new bike all afternoon if she wanted to. She could ride her bike forever and never come back.

CHAPTER TWENTY-FOUR

Asia coasted across the railroad tracks and down a short steep slope to the public beach. She wheeled her bike onto the baking sand, past the long line of people at the concession stand. The smell of French fries and hamburgers wafted over her. She wasn't hungry, but she wished she had brought some money to buy a Coke. She sat on a log and dug the toes of her runners into the hot sand.

The beach was crowded. People sunbathed on towels and tossed Frisbees back and forth. Little kids dug in the sand and clambered on the logs. A man and a boy were even swimming, which surprised her. She was sure the ocean was polluted in a big city like Vancouver.

Just then a gray cat leaped out of nowhere and crouched on the end of her log, its slanted amber eyes fixed on her in an unblinking stare.

"Hello, cat," said Asia.

The cat marched along the log until it was close enough for Asia to touch. It was a big cat, with thick smoky fur. She reached out to stroke its head, and it batted her hand with a soft paw.

"I think you want to play," said Asia. She looked around for something to dangle in front of the cat. Remembering her Saint Christopher medal, she slipped it over her head and swung it gently back and forth.

The cat followed the motion with its eyes. Asia, filled with a sudden longing, found herself missing Dandy all over again. She wondered if the cat was a stray and whether she could take it back to Beth's house.

Whoosh! The cat pounced and swiped the chain with its paw, yanking it out of Asia's hand. It jumped off the log and streaked up the beach, the chain dangling from its mouth.

"Hey!" cried Asia. For a stunned second, she didn't move. She had never seen a cat do anything like that before. Then panic swept over her, and she chased the cat across the sand. It darted behind the concession stand and along a strip of sidewalk, disappearing finally up a narrow road dappled with shade.

A sign said Bellevue Avenue. Asia stared along the road, willing the cat to come back. Choking back her angry sobs, she ran to the beach to get her bike.

⁓

Asia rode along shady tree-lined Bellevue Avenue, past huge houses behind stone walls and fancy iron gates. The houses were even bigger than Beth's. Some of them looked more like hotels. On one side of the road, between the houses, glimpses of blue ocean sparkled in the sun, and on the other, blackberry bushes grew in a tangle beside the railroad tracks. She fought back the rising panic that welled inside her. The cat could be anywhere by now. It could have dropped her medal in a ditch or in the bushes.

Asia skidded to a stop.

The gray cat was in full view, crouching on the pavement in front of a high fence covered in leafy green vines. Its amber eyes watched her. The silver medal and chain dangled from its mouth. It flicked its tail. Asia felt like it was looking right inside her brain. Hardly daring to breathe, she laid her bike on the ground and stretched out her hand. "Here, kitty."

The cat leaped onto the fence, its claws scrabbling for a grip in the thick vines, and disappeared over the top. Asia crossed the road. The vines smothered the fence in a thick green tangled mat. The fence looked too shabby and wild for Bellevue Avenue. She pulled back some of the leaves to see if she could peer inside, but the old boards underneath were too close together. She stepped back and gazed up. Over the top of the fence she glimpsed dark trees and part of a mossy roof with a small round dormer window half buried in more vines.

Something gray flashed near the top of one of the trees. It was the cat, staring at her through the branches. It jumped onto the roof and slipped inside the window.

Asia studied the fence again and spotted a small wooden door partly hidden in the leaves. It had been painted blue once, but most of the paint was faded and peeling off. A black iron handle, shaped like a long thin bird, hung above a rusty keyhole. A small wooden sign, buried deep in the vines beside the door, said *Cormorant Cottage*. Asia pulled the handle gently. The door didn't budge. She pulled a few more times, harder, but it was locked tight.

She kicked the door angrily. Then she crossed to the middle of the street so she could get a better view over the high fence. Her heart jumped. An old woman with long white hair was staring through the little dormer window. For a second their eyes locked. The cat appeared again, brushing against the old woman's shoulder. Asia felt the intensity of the woman's gaze boring into her.

She let out her breath. Maybe the old woman thought Asia was trying to break in. She wished she had the nerve to go right up to the house and bang on the door and demand her medal back. But the woman in the window was too creepy. And there was something very weird about the cat, the way it kept appearing and disappearing.

She would have to think what to do next. Her runners dragging, she walked back to her bike. She climbed on the seat and took one last glance back. The window was in deep shade now, and she couldn't tell if the woman had gone or whether she was still standing there, watching her leave.

CHAPTER TWENTY-FIVE

A brown station wagon was parked in Beth's driveway when Asia got back. She glanced in the window as she wheeled her bike past. Comic books, crumpled juice boxes, a baseball cap and a Barbie were scattered across the backseat. Little kids' stuff. Ben and Sierra must be here.

Asia felt nervous about walking in the front door. She went around to the side of the house and slipped in the kitchen door instead. The kitchen smelled like Chinese food, and white cardboard take-out cartons were lined up on the counter. They must be staying for supper. Asia slid her backpack off her shoulders. Voices murmured from the living room, and she was just wondering if she could slip upstairs unseen when a small blond boy shot into the kitchen, a plastic cup in his hand. He skidded to a stop and shouted, "She's here! She's *here!*"

The kitchen filled with people. Asia recognized faces from the photographs in the den—the man and woman in the wedding picture, the little girl with freckles who had grinned in the picture but who stood now with her back pressed against the fridge, a comic clutched tightly in one hand, her face unreadable. Asia smiled stiffly while Beth made the introductions. Sam was a big athletic-looking man. Valerie was shorter and more rumpled than Beth, but she had the same smile: wide and turned up at the ends. "You've put Ben out of his agony. He's been jumping with excitement all afternoon."

"I have not," said Ben automatically. He gaped at Asia. "I forget. Is Asia my real cousin?"

"Of course she is," said Beth.

Ben frowned. "Why?"

Sierra spoke for the first time. Her voice was sharp and scornful. "How many times do we have to tell you? Asia's mother and Mom were sisters."

There was a short silence. Asia felt like everyone was staring at her. Her chest tightened and her cheeks burned. Sierra sighed. She spun a magnetic apple on the fridge door and said, "Is it okay if we watch TV until suppertime?"

Valerie looked like she was about to object, but Beth said quickly, "I think that's a very good idea."

～

Sierra slid into a big armchair in the den and chewed her fingernails. Asia sat on the floor with Ben in front of the TV cabinet. "There's lots of movies in here," she said. "What do you want to watch?"

"I know there's lots of movies," said Ben. "I come here all the time."

Asia flushed. She waited while Ben pulled DVDs out of the cupboard. He looked at each one and sighed. "*Stuart Little*," he said finally, "though I've seen it a million times." He popped the DVD out of its case. "How come you don't live with your mom and dad?"

"Shut up, Ben," said Sierra, without looking up.

"I can *ask*, can't I?" said Ben. "I'm just *asking*."

"Grandma already explained it to you." Sierra slumped lower in her chair and opened her comic book. Asia made a neat stack of the DVDs on the carpet. She saw Sierra slide her eyes toward her and then look away.

"I forget," said Ben.

"You're supposed to mind your own business," said Sierra crossly from behind her comic.

Ben slid *Stuart Little* into the DVD player and fast-forwarded it. He flopped on his stomach, his eyes fixed on the screen.

Grandma explained it to you. Asia couldn't imagine ever calling Beth Grandma. And what exactly had she said to Sierra and Ben? *You have to be nice to Asia because she's your cousin and by the way, she doesn't have any idea who her father is, and her mother abandoned her.* A lump pressed against her throat. She took a slow steadying breath.

Ben gave a sudden screech of laughter. He turned and looked at Asia. "You're not watching!"

Asia forced herself to focus on the screen. A mouse

was driving a red sports car along a city street. "There's Grandma's car!" yelled Ben.

"No it's not," said Sierra. She had closed the comic book and was staring at the TV too, her knees pulled up so they almost touched her little pointed chin.

"Yes it is," said Ben.

"That's stupid," said Sierra. "How could Grandma's car get in a movie? And it's way too small anyway. You are so dumb, Ben."

Ben frowned. "Grandma told me."

"Now you're dumb *and* a liar."

Asia shut out her cousins and closed her eyes. In the flurry of meeting everyone, she had forgotten about her Saint Christopher medal, but now its loss came back to her with a sickening jolt. What would Maddy say if she knew she had lost the medal? Tears stung the back of her eyelids, and she tried to concentrate on the movie. Maybe they could keep watching it, rewinding and starting it over and over again, until it was time for everyone to leave. But then Valerie popped her head in the doorway. "Dinner, guys. We're eating outside. Don't forget to wash your hands, and then you can help yourselves."

Asia stayed back while the others crowded around the containers of food. After she served herself, she carried her plate to the backyard and sat on the steps at the edge of the wooden deck above the lawn. Ben and Sierra argued about who got the swinging chair, until finally Sierra flung herself to one end so that Ben could share it with her. Asia's favorite restaurant in the town near Cold Creek was the

Blue Lotus. This food looked exactly the same as the food Mr. Sing made at the Blue Lotus, but for some reason the smell made her feel sick. She picked at a piece of bright red sweet-and-sour pork.

Sam and Valerie were talking about a new condominium tower that was being built somewhere near the ocean. "It would be perfect for you, Mom," said Valerie. "Instead of rattling around in this big house."

"I like rattling around in this big house," said Beth evenly. "And now Asia and I can rattle around together."

Valerie frowned and Beth changed the topic quickly. "Tell me about Ben's play camp. Is it a success?"

The evening was never going to end. Ben curled up on the grass and fell asleep. Sierra, her meal abandoned, stretched out on the swing, her legs like skinny peeled sticks. Sam buried himself in a newspaper, and Beth leaned back in her lawn chair and closed her eyes.

Valerie gathered up plates. Asia, who was used to helping Maddy, followed her inside with a tray of glasses and cutlery. Valerie rinsed dishes and passed them to Asia to load in the dishwasher.

"So, Asia, how are you getting along?" she said after a few minutes.

"Fine." Asia slid a handful of forks into the little basket. Beth had given her a dishwasher lesson that morning. Asia had never seen a kitchen that did so many things for you: a dishwasher for the dishes, a garborator for the garbage, a coffeemaker that came on automatically before Beth even got out of bed.

Asia struggled for something to say. "Beth bought me a bike."

"I know." Valerie scraped leftover noodles into the garborator. "I was a bit worried about the traffic, but Mom said Maddy told her you were very independent and sensible."

Asia's heart did a quick jump at hearing a stranger say Maddy's name so casually. She concentrated on lining up the glasses so they all fit. Valerie smiled at her. "Mom's going to love having your company."

"I'm not going to be here for very long."

It wasn't exactly a lie. For a second, Asia pretended that Maddy had called and said that Ira was getting better and they were going to stay at Cold Creek after all.

Valerie held the plate a second longer than usual under the tap. "Well, we'll make the most of it while we've got you, then. Tell me where you went today."

Asia told her about going to the library and the beach. She described Cormorant Cottage on Bellevue Avenue, but she didn't say anything about the cat taking her medal or the old woman at the window. Valerie probably wouldn't believe her anyway. "That must be one of the original old cottages," said Valerie, sounding interested. "Most of them have been torn down by developers, but I've heard there's a few of the old places left."

After that, to Asia's relief, she seemed lost in her own thoughts. Finally the others drifted back through the house to the front door, Sam holding a sleepy Ben in his arms. The phone rang and Beth disappeared for a minute. When she came back, she said, "It's for you, Asia."

Asia stared at Beth.

"It's Maddy." Beth touched Asia's shoulder. "Everything's fine. She just wants to say hello. You can take it in the den."

Asia walked to the den on wooden legs. She didn't trust herself to talk to Maddy yet. She stared at the phone for a few seconds before she picked it up.

"Please deposit another dollar," said the operator.

"Hang on a minute," said Maddy's voice. A loudspeaker in the background said, "Paging Doctor Clarke."

She was calling from the hospital. Asia gripped the phone tightly while coins jangled at the other end.

"Fiddle," said Maddy. Asia imagined her rummaging in her striped bag for change. She sucked in her breath and set the phone carefully back on the receiver. Her heart was thudding so loudly she could hear it in her ears. She turned around.

Sierra was standing in the doorway, her sharp eyes alive with curiosity. How long had the little girl been spying on her? Anger stirred inside Asia. Sierra's cheeks turned pink. "I just came back for my comic," she mumbled as she grabbed her comic book off the table beside the armchair and fled.

Asia stood very still for a few minutes. Then she slipped out of the den and quietly climbed the stairs to her room. The front door slammed, and voices drifted up from the driveway below her window. A car horn honked, Valerie called out something, and Beth laughed.

The jarring clang of the phone made her jump. It rang exactly sixteen times while she stood, her heart racing, in the middle of the room. She willed it to stop, but when it did, the silence in the house was worse—suffocating and accusing. She sank onto the bed, her hand automatically going to her neck to touch her Saint Christopher medal. Misery, mingled with fear, seeped into her like cold gray fog. Losing a Saint Christopher medal must be a powerful omen of bad luck, even danger.

She picked up Lost Rabbit and buried her face in his soft blue fur.

CHAPTER TWENTY-SIX

In the morning, Beth took Asia to the mall to look at clothes. The word *school* was everywhere: on the flyers that stood in racks at the entrances to the stores, on the bright red signs that hung in the aisles. Asia didn't want anything, but she picked out a pair of jeans and a couple of T-shirts. When they were finished, Beth suggested a drink in the restaurant at the end of the mall.

When they went inside, a small hand waved excitedly from the far wall. Valerie, Sam and Sierra were in the back corner, squeezed around a small table cluttered with soup bowls and plates of half-eaten sandwiches. There was a minute of confusion while Sam found two more chairs and Valerie moved dishes around to clear space. "Ben's at a birthday party," she explained. "Bowling *and* swimming, which is ridiculous. He'll be so cranky when he gets home."

"You baby him too much," said Sam. "He'll be fine. Now what can I get for you ladies?"

Beth smiled. "Coffee for me, thanks. Asia and I gave ourselves the luxury of sleeping in, and we've just had a big breakfast."

Asia went up to the counter with Sam, and he recited all the choices as enthusiastically as if he had cooked them himself—shepherd's pie, cabbage rolls, ham and cheese quiche. "I'd like a smoothie," she said, but Sam insisted on adding a blueberry muffin for Beth and a Danish for her.

She had half-heartedly broken off a piece of bun when Sierra blurted out, "Daddy, Asia has *her* ears pierced!"

Valerie said, "Sierra, don't start—," but it was too late. Sam had picked up a newspaper that someone had left on the next table. He put it down and peered at Sierra.

A stubborn look spread across Sierra's face. "If Asia can have pierced ears, why can't I?"

Sam sighed. "How old are you, Asia?"

"Twelve," said Asia.

"Okay," said Sam. "Sierra, you can get your ears pierced when you're twelve."

Sierra's eyes narrowed. "But that doesn't mean Asia *got* them when she was twelve! She could have—"

"Thirteen," said Sam. "Fourteen if you keep whining."

Sierra burst into tears, and two teenage girls at a nearby table stared at them. Asia wished she could sink into the floor.

"Fifteen," said Sam.

"For heaven's sake, Sam," said Valerie sharply. "Sierra, stop it."

Sam stood up. His eyes were cold. "Pardon me if I don't believe in self-mutilation for my daughter. I've got a squash court booked for two o'clock."

They watched Sam wind his way through the tables and out the door without a backward glance.

"He doesn't believe in what?" said Asia.

"Self-mutilation," said Valerie. "Poking holes in your body." She smiled wearily.

"It's not funny," said Sierra. Her tears had turned off like a tap, and she was glaring at her mother. "I'm the only one in the whole school—"

"Mom, we're going to go. Sorry about the fuss. Come on, Sierra, let's go get your supplies so you won't be the only one in the whole school without a pencil."

It was quiet after they left, the tables around them emptying as the noon rush died down. Asia wondered if Beth had planned the rest of her day for her. She looked at the blob of rubbery red jelly in the middle of her Danish and sighed. "I can't eat this."

"I'm not surprised," said Beth. "I don't know why Sam always insists on ordering all this food." She gathered up her parcels. "I love them all dearly but they exhaust me. A quiet afternoon of writing is starting to sound tempting. How about if we go home?"

Home was Cold Creek. Asia didn't say anything.

"Do you think you could entertain yourself for the afternoon?"

Asia pushed away her thoughts of Maddy and Ira. "Yes," she said quickly, "I can."

～

Asia sat on a bench on Marine Drive, sipping from her water bottle and watching a man water a hanging basket of pink and white flowers. She was thinking about getting back on her bike when a sudden movement on the sidewalk in front of the grocery store caught her eye. A gray cat rolled over on its back on the pavement. It jumped up and stretched its front legs against the concrete wall. Asia recognized it right away. It was the same cat who had taken her Saint Christopher medal. She studied it for a minute, then stood up and walked over to it. She bent down and put out her hand. "Hello, cat. You're a long way from home."

No one would ever believe that this cat had stolen her medal and carried it away in its mouth. Asia wouldn't believe it if she hadn't seen it with her own eyes. She thought she should hate the cat, but she didn't. It stared at her without blinking, and she had an eerie feeling that it was looking right inside her head again. It scooted away from her hand and darted across the street between two moving cars. Frowning slightly, she watched it disappear across the railroad tracks.

On the store wall, right above the spot where the cat had stretched, was a large bulletin board. Asia finished her water while she read the notices. Someone was giving pottery lessons at the community center, a springer spaniel called Winston had gone missing, and an art show was opening at the Dolphin Gallery. She had just decided to leave when a notice jumped out at her, underneath the photograph of Winston. It was a little card, yellowed and old looking, with spidery black writing.

> *Wanted*
> *A twelve-year-old girl with a bike to do an odd*
> *job. Apply to Mary Wintergreen. Cormorant Cottage.*
> *Bellevue Avenue.*

Asia felt a jolt of surprise. Cormorant Cottage was the name of the funny place with the old fence where the gray cat lived. She read the notice again. It made her feel strange. She was a twelve-year-old girl with a bike. Mary Wintergreen must be the name of the old lady who had stared at her from the little window in the roof. She probably meant *to do odd jobs*, thought Asia. Her handwriting was shaky. She had mixed up the part about odd jobs, and she had forgotten to put a street number. She must be *very* old.

Asia didn't want a job, but she did want to get inside Cormorant Cottage. Just once, so she could get her Saint Christopher medal back.

She slid her water bottle back in its holder and unchained her bike from the rack. She crossed the street, coasted across the railroad tracks and turned onto Bellevue Avenue.

Asia rode past all the fancy houses as far as the old vine-covered fence. She got off her bike and studied it. It didn't seem creepy today, just sleepy and peaceful in the afternoon sun.

A white pickup truck with the words *Green Umbrella Gardening Service* on the side was parked at the top of the driveway next door. Two men with dark tans sat on the open tailgate drinking cans of pop.

"If you're selling cookies or something, you're wasting your time," said one of the men with a grin. "Nobody lives there."

Asia ignored the gardeners. She walked up to the blue door in the middle of the fence. She scraped back some of the vines and read the little wooden sign. *Cormorant Cottage.* She took a big breath and pulled the black iron handle shaped like a bird. This time, with a creak of its rusty hinges, the blue door swung open.

CHAPTER TWENTY=SEVEN

Asia wheeled her bike through the blue door into a cool green world. The fence enclosed both sides of the narrow property, all the way to the ocean. Huge evergreen trees with dark droopy branches hid the sun. A path of crumbling mossy bricks wound through long grass to the front door of a small house with a peaked roof. The house was smothered in such a thick blanket of ivy that the two dark leaded windows on either side of the door looked like eyes peering at her through the green leaves.

Asia leaned her bike against the inside of the fence. It had seemed like a good idea to come here, but now a knot of apprehension filled her stomach. If it wasn't for her medal, she would go right back out. Slowly she walked along the path. She hesitated in front of the door, then took a big breath and knocked.

There was no sound from inside the house. She pressed her face against one of the windows. Something moved in the shadows; it was the gray cat jumping onto the window-sill. It stared at Asia through the glass and then disappeared. Asia gave one final knock and turned away from the door. She walked around the side of the house, squeezing past a tangle of bushes and stepping over an old ladder that lay in the weeds. The front of the property was open to the ocean, separated from a strip of rocky beach by a low stone wall. The tide was a long way out. A black bird stood on top of a rock that poked out of the water, his wings stuck out on either side like a giant bat. A man and a small brown spaniel were picking their way across the seaweed-strewn rocks. Two seagulls hopped along the wall, fighting over a piece of orange crab shell.

The ivy had given up on this side of the cottage, maybe because of the ocean winds, and only a few vines clung to the brown shingles and the railings of a rickety porch. A large blue glass ball propped open a screen door. Asia climbed up the porch steps and stood by the open door. She peered into a narrow dark hallway. Her heart thudded. "Hello," she called. "Is anyone home?"

For a minute the only sound was the screeching of the seagulls, and then she heard the soft *pad pad pad* of foot-steps in the dim hallway. An old woman stepped into the doorway. She was tall, with a deeply wrinkled face; her hair was snowy white and coiled at the back of her neck. She was wearing a faded blue cotton dress and bedroom slippers.

"Hello, dear," she said softly.

Asia tried to still the thumping of her heart. She had never done anything like this in her life, and she was sure that Beth would disapprove. "I'm Asia Cumfrey. I'm here about the notice at the store."

"I am very pleased you have come." There was a tremor in the old woman's voice, but her gaze was steady. "My name is Mary Wintergreen."

There was a long silence. Asia shifted uncomfortably. She wished the woman would stop staring at her. "I was wondering what a cormorant is," she said, partly to break the silence.

"Why, it's a bird," said the woman. She pointed to the black bird on the rock. "I see them every day."

Asia looked at the motionless bird with the huge outspread wings. "Why does it just stand there? What's it doing?"

"Drying its wings in the sun," said Mary Wintergreen. "It has to do that after it's been fishing, or else it can't fly."

"Oh," said Asia.

"I'll bring the tea out." The old woman brushed Asia's arm with a thin cold hand. "You sit here and wait."

There was an old armchair and a wooden rocking chair on the porch. Asia dropped into the soft squishy armchair. She didn't feel quite so nervous. After all, nothing could happen to her out here. She lifted her heavy hair off the back of her neck. She sighed. It was so hot. She hoped Mary Wintergreen would bring iced tea.

The old woman was gone for ages. The man and the dog had disappeared, and the beach was quiet. The cormorant turned its head; otherwise it looked just like a statue. She was wondering how long it would stay there and if its wings ached, when the gray cat rubbed up against her legs.

"Hello there," she said. "Where did you come from?" She patted his back and studied him closely. His gold eyes blinked lazily.

"I see you've met Monty." Mary Wintergreen padded onto the porch, carrying a tray with a teapot and two teacups decorated with rosebuds. She set the tray on a low wicker table and sat beside Asia in the rocking chair. She poured the tea, her hands trembling so badly the cups rattled on their saucers.

Asia took a sip. The tea was scalding and bitter. She put her cup on the table and gathered up her courage. "I have to know what you want me to do before I agree to anything."

Mary Wintergreen stared at her, her pale green eyes unblinking.

"I mean," stammered Asia, "what exactly are the odd jobs?"

"Didn't you read my card?" said the old woman. " I said an odd *job*, not *jobs*."

"But I thought—"

Mary Wintergreen hadn't touched her tea. "I want you to find something."

Asia blinked. For a second she thought the woman meant her Saint Christopher medal. "What do you mean? Find what?"

The rocking chair creaked back and forth. The old woman closed her eyes. Strands of wispy white hair blew gently around her face.

"Find what?" Asia repeated in a louder voice.

She studied the wrinkled face. She's fallen asleep, Asia thought incredulously. She waited a few minutes and then pushed herself out of the armchair and walked softly down the porch steps. Part of her was sorry she hadn't had a chance to look for her medal and part of her was glad to escape.

"Come back tomorrow in the afternoon. We'll start then."

The voice was no more than a whisper. Asia spun around. The rocking chair was empty, and the screen door closed with a faint click.

"I might come back and I might not," she said to the closed door.

She looked out at the ocean. The cormorant had flown away when she wasn't looking, and she felt disappointed that she had missed it. She sighed and walked around the side of the cottage and up the path through the trees. She got her bike and went back out through the fence. The two gardeners were loading tools into the back of their truck. They peered at her closely, as if she had been up to no good. Asia flushed. "You were wrong, actually. Someone does live here. I've met her and we've just had tea."

She rode back down Bellevue Avenue to the grocery store at the corner. She wanted to have one more look at Mary Wintergreen's notice before going back to the house. She scanned the bulletin board in front of the grocery store in confusion. The card with the spidery printing was gone.

A boy wearing a green apron was taking down the notice about the art show. "Looking for something?" he said cheerfully.

Asia said slowly, "There was a card here, just a little while ago, but it's gone. It had very wiggly black printing on it. And it was old."

"Old? I don't think so. I'm in charge of the bulletin board. I change the notices every three weeks, and I would've remembered a card like that."

"Maybe someone put it up without telling you," said Asia.

The boy looked shocked. "I would've known. All the notices go through me. They have to be date stamped. After three weeks, I take them down. That way everyone gets a turn."

"Well it *was* here," persisted Asia. "It was right under this picture of the missing dog."

Asia and the boy both stared at a green poster advertising a skateboard sale that filled the space below the missing spaniel's photograph. The boy squinted at the date stamped in the corner. "That one's been there for over ten days. I remember putting it up."

Whistling, he went back inside the store. Asia's cheeks felt hot. He thought she had made up the little card with the spidery writing. Just like the gardeners thought she had made up having tea at Cormorant Cottage. But she hadn't. She knew these things had happened to her. What she didn't know was why.

She started the steep hot climb to Beth's house. She got off her bike and walked the last two blocks. By that time, she had made two decisions. First, she was going to go back to Cormorant Cottage. Second, she was not going to tell Beth.

CHAPTER TWENTY-EIGHT

In the morning, Asia's throat felt scratchy and it hurt to swallow. Her blanket was crumpled at the bottom of the bed, and she reached down and tugged it over her shoulders. It was her third morning waking up in Sherri's old bedroom, and she still wasn't used to it.

Beth had said she could fix the room up, but Asia wasn't interested. She wasn't planning on staying. She rolled onto her side and looked at her old stuffed rabbits. It was easy to pretend that the expressions on Lucky Rabbit's and Boy Rabbit's worn faces were full of reproach. They didn't like it here either.

Asia had never thought about where her rabbits had come from; they were just something that she had owned forever. But now she wondered if her mother had bought them for her, just like she had bought the new bunny. She studied Lost Rabbit's plush blue face and tried to imagine Sherri picking him out in a store somewhere in Alberta or Saskatchewan.

She tested her throat. It was hot and dry, and a big lump got in the way when she tried to swallow. The water glass beside her bed was empty, and she sat up and slid her feet onto the floor.

The phone rang. Three long trills.

Maddy never phoned in the morning. Asia frowned, unsure whether to stay up or crawl back into bed. The house was silent. At first she felt relieved, and then a tiny thread of worry niggled at her. What if it *had* been Maddy and something had happened to Ira in the night?

Asia found Beth in the kitchen, sitting at the table with a cup of tea. Beth's face was pale, and the worry in Asia erupted into panic. "Is Ira okay?"

Her grandmother smiled, but her eyes were distant. "He's fine. I didn't know you were up. You startled me."

"Was that Maddy?'

"No, it wasn't. Sit down and I'll make some toast."

"I don't want any toast." Asia slid into a chair. Her throat felt like it was on fire.

"Tea?"

Asia shook her head.

Beth refilled her own cup. "That was someone called Gina on the phone," she said quietly.

Asia wished she had stayed in bed. Her head felt wooly, and it took her a few seconds to understand what her grandmother was telling her.

"Right after I talked to Harry, I put a notice in two Winnipeg newspapers asking for any information about you and Sherri. Harry told me your birth certificate says that you were born in Winnipeg." Beth hesitated. "I had no idea Sherri had gone there. It seems so far away."

Asia traced her fingers around a flower on the patterned tablecloth. She wished Beth would stop talking.

"I thought I might finally find out what had happened, maybe find someone who had met Sherri." Beth's voice was soft and steady, and the color had returned to her face. "And now this woman called Gina has phoned. She knew your mother and she knew you."

Asia's hand stilled and she stared at Beth.

"She and her sister were your neighbors in a trailer park when you were a baby. Before you came to Cold Creek. She remembers you well. She used to look after you when Sherri went to work." Beth stood up and carried her cup to the sink. "Gina lives in Vancouver now, but her sister still lives in Winnipeg, and she saw my notice and phoned her." There was a tiny pause. "I've asked Gina to come and meet us."

The room gave a slight spin. Asia was freezing. The cold was seeping right up through her bare feet, which was odd because her back was prickling with sweat. She stood up on wobbly legs and was only dimly aware of her grandmother spinning around, instant concern spreading across her face.

"My throat hurts," whispered Asia. "I feel awful."

～

Beth sent Asia back to bed and brought her a mug of warm

water and honey and a spoon to sip it with. "My girls always said it worked better that way," she said.

My girls. She meant Sherri and Valerie. The soothing liquid trickled down Asia's throat. She curled up under her blanket and in a few minutes drifted back to sleep. In the afternoon, Beth gave her apple juice and a boiled egg and then took her to the medical clinic on Marine Drive. "It's strep throat," said Beth when they left the doctor's office. "You won't be going anywhere for awhile. You stay in the car while I run down to the drugstore and pick up this prescription."

Asia worried that the old woman on Bellevue Avenue would give the job to someone else if she didn't go back right away, but Beth was firm that she had to stay inside. For the next three days Asia slept, watched all the movies in the cabinet in the den and started working through her stack of library books. One afternoon, Beth brought out a thick family photo album, and they sat together at the kitchen table and flipped through the pages. Asia found it exhausting to concentrate on all the faces. It was hard to feel anything for any of them, even the slim girl with black hair who looked like her but was a complete stranger, and whose photos filled many pages and then disappeared. Beth obviously expected her to ask a lot of questions, but she couldn't think of anything to say, and after awhile Beth fell silent too. "We're getting into Sierra and Ben's baby pictures," she said finally. "We'll save that for another day." Asia escaped thankfully to her book.

Maddy phoned every evening, and Asia listened to Beth's reassurances. "She's fine…Yes, she got a little overtired, I think. A lot of stress." She hated it when they talked about her like that. She glued her eyes to her book when Beth said, "I told Maddy that as soon as your throat is better, and it doesn't hurt to talk, you'll call her."

When she woke up on Saturday morning, the house was quiet. There was a note on the kitchen counter. *I'm at Val's. Be back soon. Custard in fridge. Beth.* Asia ate a bowl of custard standing at the counter then she wandered through the big silent house. Her sore throat had finally gone away, and the tiredness of the last few days faded to boredom. It was the first time she had been alone in the house. Beth spent a lot of time in her computer room, but she always kept the door open, and now Asia missed the *tap tap tap* of her keyboard.

She stood in the doorway of the little room now and peered around curiously. The rest of the house was so tidy that sometimes it looked like no one lived in it, but this room was messy. Papers were scattered across a big round table and Asia counted four abandoned mugs. Little yellow Post-it notes with scrawled messages dotted the wall around the computer. Beth never talked about the book she was writing, and Asia only knew that it required a lot of research and that there was some deadline looming. She walked into the room and picked up a magazine that lay on the seat of a chair. A bold black title said *Supernatural* and underneath was a picture of a foggy street with a pale green light glowing at the end. Asia flipped open to the first page, and a name in the table of contents jumped out at her. Beth Cumfrey.

She read the title of the article beside her grandmother's name. *Ghost Encounters: The Genetic Link.* She had no idea what it meant. She found the article and scanned the first paragraph, but it was full of scientific-sounding words, and she couldn't concentrate. She put the magazine down and glanced at the computer screen, where the screen saver's tropical fish swam lazily by. She walked over to the computer and pressed a key, and a little sign popped up—*You have eleven new messages.* It looked like Beth got a lot of e-mail.

There was a large pile of printed pages beside the computer. Asia picked up the paper on top and read out loud: *I am e-mailing you in response to your request for true stories of ghost encounters within families. I think that it's a fascinating topic for a book and I have a story you might be interested in*—Her grandmother was writing a book about ghosts! What would she say if she knew that Asia had seen a ghost, not once but twice? She hadn't even told Maddy about the ghost at the Old Farm, and in the upheaval of the move she had almost forgotten about it. Now the images came back to her vividly: the eerie form hovering on the stairs of the old house, the tall woman crying on the bridge.

Why was her grandmother so interested in ghosts? Asia's eyes flickered over the titles of the books on the shelf beside the computer. *True Ghost Encounters. Ghost Stories of British Columbia. Ghosts and the Gold Rush. Haunted.* A key rattled in the front door and, a second later, parcels thumped on the hall floor. Asia dropped the paper back on the pile and slipped out of the room.

CHAPTER TWENTY-NINE

"I brought Sierra back with me," said Beth. "You're not contagious anymore and she needs a break."

A break from what? Asia stared at her cousin in dismay. She was pressed up against the hall wall, her thin face pinched in its usual frown.

"Sierra and I did a big shop. How about if you two bring in the rest of the bags? Then I'll make us some sandwiches, and maybe you girls could find a board game to play." Beth peered closely at Asia. "You're looking much better."

"I feel fine," muttered Asia. Beth was treating her as if she were a little kid. Resentment flooded through her. She had been planning to ask if she could go for a bike ride today. The old woman at Cormorant Cottage would think she had forgotten all about the job by now, and she would never get her Saint Christopher medal back.

"Maddy called last night," said Beth when Asia set the last bag on the counter. "Ira has developed a mild pneumonia."

Asia froze. Why had Beth waited so long to tell her? "Is Maddy worried?"

Sierra's sharp eyes flashed back and forth between Asia and Beth. "It's always a little bit of a worry when someone Ira's age gets sick," said Beth calmly. "Especially after a heart attack. But it's not unusual for old people to get pneumonia when they're in the hospital."

"Why?" said Sierra.

"I don't know. I think there's a lot of germs in a hospital, which sounds silly doesn't it? Or maybe they just get a bit weak. Anyway it means he'll have to stay in the hospital a little longer than they thought."

It didn't sound too serious. Asia watched Sierra stack cans in a wobbly pyramid. "Sierra, honey, you're making more work, not less," said Beth, but she was smiling.

Sierra sighed. "Can I see your room, Asia?"

"I guess so," said Asia.

Sierra climbed up the stairs ahead of Asia and surveyed the little bedroom with a disappointed look on her face. "Where's all your stuff?"

Asia shrugged. "I didn't bring much. I'm not going to be staying here for very long."

"But Grandma said—"

At that moment, Sierra spotted the bunnies. She picked up each one separately and pressed it against her face. "Mmm…they're soft." Her voice lowered. "Mom's really mad at Dad."

"Oh," said Asia. Why was Sierra looking at her like that? She couldn't care less if Sam and Valerie were having a fight. The room was stuffy and hot. She walked over to the window and pushed it open. She looked at the mountains and wished she were by herself. She thought about Ira. Did it hurt to have pneumonia?

"He didn't come home last night," said Sierra.

"Who?" said Asia. She studied the giant tree in the corner of the yard. You would be able to see a long way from the top of that tree.

"My dad. He went to Uncle Steve's apartment. Mom says she doesn't care if he stays there forever."

Asia turned away from the window reluctantly. Sierra's eyes searched her face. "It's not fair."

"I don't know," said Asia weakly.

"It's *not*. Ben and I want him to come home but Mom doesn't. She said not *ever*."

"She probably doesn't mean that."

"Yes she does."

Asia swallowed. Sierra had abandoned the bunnies and was wandering around the room. She stopped beside Ira's wolf box and stroked its smooth satiny sides. "This is beautiful," she said softly.

Asia frowned. She didn't want Sierra to find the secret drawer. She couldn't bear the thought of her curious fingers touching her stone and her four-leaf clover.

"Come on," she said. "I'm going to show you something outside."

～

Sierra stood under the tree and peered high up into the leafy branches. "I can't."

"Yes you can," said Asia. "I'll boost you onto the first branch, and then I'll come up right behind you."

"What if I fall?"

"You won't. I promise."

Sierra still didn't move. "Are we going to tell Grandma?"

"No," said Asia. "Grown-ups worry about this kind of thing too much. Come on. Reach up and grab that branch."

Sierra stretched up on her tiptoes. Asia wrapped her arms around Sierra's skinny legs and heaved her up with a grunt. Sierra clung onto the branch like a monkey, her eyes fixed on Asia, who scrambled nimbly up beside her. Asia craned her neck back and studied the tree. "That was the hardest part. The rest is going to be easy, just like climbing a ladder. You go first and I'll follow you."

Sierra hesitated and then started to climb. She made soft panting noises as she pulled herself from branch to branch. Up and up the girls climbed through the leafy green tree, in and out of the patches of dappled sun and cool shade. Finally Asia said, "This is far enough. Don't look down until we get settled."

She showed Sierra how to wiggle into the crook of the tree, leaning her back against the massive trunk, and then she found a spot for herself. She parted the leafy curtain in front of them and said, "Now we can look."

A thrill ran through Asia as she swept her eyes over the rooftops of the neighboring houses. The mountains looked closer, the sky bluer from up here. It was a wonderful climbing tree, almost as good as the one at Cold Creek. "We can see the ocean," breathed Sierra after a minute of raptured silence.

"I knew we would," said Asia triumphantly. She gazed at the distant strip of dazzling blue water. "One day I'm going to put a message in a bottle and send it on that ocean all the way to California."

"Can I send one too?" said Sierra.

"Maybe," said Asia. "Why not?" She picked a leaf off the branch in front of her and let it drop, watching it twirl in the air.

Beside her, Sierra sucked in her breath. "Grandma!"

Asia peeked through the branches and watched Beth close the back door and stand on the deck. "Keep still," she whispered. But Beth had seen them. She walked across the lawn and stood under the tree. Her tanned face peered up at them through the silvery leaves. Asia's chest tightened. But Beth was smiling, a huge smile that spread right across her face.

"When you two are ready to come down, lunch is ready," she called up. "And by the way, don't think you're the first clever ones to think of climbing this tree. Your mothers used to do it too, just to scare the daylights out of me."

Sierra laughed. "Did it work?"

"Every single time. Where do you think I got all this gray hair?"

CHAPTER THIRTY

Asia munched on a tuna-fish sandwich and watched her grandmother through the kitchen window, picking dead flowers off a bed of daisies. The day was flying by, and soon it would be too late to go back to Cormorant Cottage.

"What are we going to do next?" said Sierra. Purple juice stained her mouth, and her freckles were vivid against her pale skin.

"Nothing." Asia fought back a pang of sympathy and hardened her voice. "I have to go out for awhile."

"Can I come?"

"No."

Sierra frowned. "Why not?"

"Because I have to ride my bike to get there."

"We could walk over to my house and get *my* bike."

Asia's heart sank. This was going to be harder than she

thought. Sierra looked stubborn and, anyway, Beth probably expected Asia to entertain her for the rest of the day.
She sighed. She had no idea what Mary Wintergreen would
say if she brought her cousin.

"Are you allowed to ride on the road?" she said finally.

"I *would* be if I was with you."

Asia hesitated. She could tell Beth they were going to the
library to return her books. They could do that first, and
then it wouldn't be a lie. She studied Sierra's hopeful face.
"Can you keep a secret?"

"From Grandma again?"

Asia felt her cheeks redden. "Yes."

"I *promise* I won't tell."

Asia gave in. "Okay, you can come."

⁓

Beth looked at Sierra doubtfully when Asia told her that
they were going to hang around the library for awhile and
read books, but after a quick phone call to Valerie she said
that Sierra could go. Asia understood the look on Beth's
face better when they got to the library. While she picked
out a new stack of mysteries, Sierra rearranged the pillows
in the little kids' reading corner and then played on one of
the computers.

"I hate reading," she told Asia when they were back outside with their bikes.

"Well I *love* reading," said Asia. She slid the books into
her backpack. "We're going somewhere else now, anyway.
Stay right behind me and be careful around the cars."

They rode back along Marine Drive and then turned up

Bellevue Avenue, Sierra clanging her bike bell every few minutes. Asia felt a moment of panic that the little blue door in the fence would be locked again, but it opened with a soft creak. They leaned their bikes against the inside of the fence and walked through the shady overgrown yard and around the side of the cottage to the ocean. The tide was in and the waves pounded against the stone wall. Asia looked for the big black cormorant, but it wasn't there today.

Mary Wintergreen was sitting on the porch, the tray with the rosebud teapot and teacups on the wicker table beside her, the gray cat asleep in her lap.

"Hello!" said Asia. "This is my cousin, Sierra. I brought her because she's good at finding things." She had no idea if that was true, but the old woman was watching them so intently.

Sierra had been silent ever since they walked through the little blue door. She stood very close to Asia. The cat jumped down and rubbed against her legs.

"Its name is Monty," said Asia.

"Would you like tea, Sierra?" said Mary Wintergreen, leaning forward and staring at her face.

"No thank you," whispered Sierra.

"Then it's time to get started." Mary Wintergreen's voice shook. "I thought you weren't coming back. We'll go into the parlor, and I'll tell you what I want you to do."

Sierra was frozen to the porch, and Asia swallowed her own nervousness and said firmly, "Come on, Sierra." They followed the old woman into the cottage. An oil lamp on a small shelf cast a dim light down a narrow hallway covered with pale mauve flowered wallpaper. As they walked down the hall, Asia caught glimpses through half open doorways of a dark kitchen with a big stone sink and a cracked linoleum floor, and a bathroom with a huge claw-foot bathtub.

The parlor was at the end of the hall, at what she supposed was really the front of the cottage. It was a small room filled with an odd assortment of chairs, a stiff couch, a table with fancy curved legs and a big black piano. Heavy crimson curtains covered the windows. Asia and Sierra sat on the couch, and Mary Wintergreen sat opposite them on a green velvet chair.

Asia glanced around the room hopefully. Her heart sank as she eyed the tall shelves that covered three of the walls, shelves filled with a jumble of books, ornaments, glass bottles, shells and other bits and pieces of clutter. The cat probably went everywhere. There were hundreds of places her Saint Christopher medal could be in all this mess.

"I want you to find a diary," said Mary Wintergreen.

A diary? This was the odd job, looking for some old diary? What a weird thing to put up a notice about. "Whose diary is it?" said Asia.

"Your young eyes are much sharper than my old ones," said Mary Wintergreen, ignoring Asia. "And I *must* find it."

"We could start with those books," said Asia doubtfully. "Maybe it's tucked in among them somewhere."

Mary Wintergreen frowned. "No, no, no. In here? No, no." She closed her eyes, and Asia was afraid she was going to fall asleep again. "The attic," she muttered. "I think she might have put it in the attic."

She opened her eyes. "There are a lot of old boxes in the attic," she said clearly. And there's the old steamer chest and the trunks. You could start there."

Asia thought that this was beginning to sound like a lot of work. Mary Wintergreen stood up quickly, and the girls followed her back into the hall to a door with a funny glass doorknob. Mary Wintergreen opened it, and Asia peered up a steep flight of stairs.

"Do you have a flashlight?" she said.

Behind her, Sierra whispered, "She's gone."

Asia glanced back down the empty hallway. Far away, the flame in the oil lamp flickered. She looked at Sierra's frightened eyes and swallowed. "We'll just go up and have a look around," she whispered. "We don't have to stay if we don't want to."

They climbed the stairs slowly to a landing with a locked door on either side and a third door that opened onto yet another flight of stairs. A dim light shone at the top. These stairs were narrower and steeper and ended at a small room with a low slanted ceiling. The light came from a wide-open round window, made of tiny panes of leaded glass. It was the little window that the cat had slipped through when he took her medal. The window where the old lady had appeared.

Sierra ran to look. "You can see our bikes!" Asia gazed over Sierra's shoulder into the shady yard with the enormous evergreen trees.

Vines had grown around the windowsill so thickly that it was like looking through a leafy green wreath. Their bikes, leaning against the old fence, looked very out of place.

The cat could have dropped her medal somewhere in this little room. She thought about telling Sierra and then changed her mind. The little girl would think she was crazy. Asia's sense of helplessness grew as she scanned the floor with its accumulation of old cardboard boxes, broken kitchen chairs, a lamp, a rolled-up carpet, a big wooden crate that might be the steamer chest, two trunks with curved tops and a tall dresser with narrow drawers. Cobwebs hung in the corners, and a thin sheet of dust coated everything.

Asia sighed. It would look odd if they didn't at least pretend to look for the diary. "Let's start with the cardboard boxes." She slid a big box with dented corners and a sagging top into the middle of the room. She knelt in front of it and tugged back the flaps. "Oh!" she gasped.

A pale white face and two glassy black eyes stared up at them.

Sierra screamed.

CHAPTER THIRTY-ONE

"It's just a doll," said Asia.

She picked it up carefully. It was sewn out of a soft material that felt like flannel. The eyes were two black buttons, and the mouth and nose were stitched with faded pink thread. It hung limply in her hands, the stuffing seeping out of one of the legs.

"Somebody loved this doll a lot," she said. "You can tell."

"That old thing?" Her fear forgotten, Sierra peered again into the box. It was full of long old-fashioned dresses folded neatly between sheets of paper. Asia put the doll down and lifted out each dress and held it up—a plain black one with pearl buttons, a blue dress with lace, and a deep red velvet one. A soft sweet scent filled the air and bits of pale mauve dried flowers drifted to the floor. "That's lavender," she said. "Maddy grows it in her garden."

Sierra stroked the velvet. "Are they costumes?"

"I don't think so. I think they're real dresses that someone wore a long time ago."

Asia folded the dresses carefully and put them back in the box. She dragged out a few more boxes from the corners of the attic, and she and Sierra dug through them. They sorted through a collection of old spoons, a wooden case full of coins, some glass bottles and a box of funny-looking pipes. In one box was a lace tablecloth, yellowed with age, and in another high laced boots that reminded Asia of the boot she had found at the Old Farm. But there was no diary.

A heavy box full of old books seemed promising at first. Sierra handed each book to Asia. She thumbed through the pages quickly and then put them in a stack beside her. The books had dark covers and looked very dull, and their musty pages made both girls sneeze. Asia's hands felt grimy, and dirt was smeared across Sierra's cheek.

Sierra gave a bored sigh. She wandered over to the little round window. "Hey! The cat's climbing up the vines!" She stuck her head right out. "Come on, Monty! You can do it!"

There was a wild scrabbling noise. The cat leaped through the window past Sierra and landed with a thump on the floor. He turned his back to the girls and washed his face.

Sierra knelt down and stroked his back. Asia watched silently. After a minute, Sierra stood up. "Can we go now?"

Asia pulled her eyes away from the cat. "Okay," she said slowly.

Asia and Sierra walked back down the two flights of stairs. Monty slid softly through their legs and darted ahead.

He pushed against a door on the other side of the hall and disappeared.

He wants me to follow him, thought Asia. "Just a minute," she said. She followed Monty through the door. She was in somebody's bedroom. The walls were papered with pale pink roses, and faded green curtains had been pulled over the windows. Everything in the room was old fashioned—a big four-poster bed covered in a pale green quilt, a dressing table, and a washstand with a blue and white basin and jug. In the corner of the room, Monty stared down at her from the top of an old wardrobe with a large beveled mirror on the door.

"Monty's a good jumper," said Sierra from the doorway.

Asia didn't say anything. She gazed around the room curiously. The walls were bare except for a photograph in an oval frame that hung over the dressing table. She walked over and studied it. The photograph was a faded brown and it looked old. It was a picture of a little girl sitting on a straight-backed chair on a porch. She was wearing a sundress and short socks and shoes with buckles, and her straight dark hair hung to her shoulders. A large cat sat on her lap.

Asia frowned. There was something oddly familiar about the photograph. She lifted it off the wall carefully and turned it over. A piece of faded brown paper, tattered at the edges, had been glued onto the back. Across the top someone had written in black ink *Daisy 1915*.

Daisy. That was the name on the little pink bed in the bedroom at the Old Farm. She turned the picture over and studied it. A jolt ran through her. She recognized it now. It was the house at the Old Farm, before the porch had collapsed.

"Come *on*, Asia," said Sierra. "I don't like it here. I want to go."

"Wait." Asia had noticed a faint ridge under the thin brown paper, from one side of the frame right across to the other. There was a tear in the bottom corner, and she poked her finger into the hole and touched the edge of something. She slid her finger back in the tear and eased it along the side of the frame. The glue was old, and a small section of the brown paper separated from the edge of the frame easily. Her heart racing, she slid out a piece of folded yellowed newspaper. She spread it open carefully, trying not to tear the worn creases. She read the faded words with a sense of disbelief.

Drowning at Cold Creek

On June 20, George Williams of Cold Creek Ranch found the body of a man drowned in the swollen waters half a mile above his homestead. Williams identified the body as his hired hand, Ridley Blackmore. A short service was held on June 22, attended by Williams, his wife Miranda and a few curious bystanders. Miranda Williams said that Blackmore was a bachelor with no family.

It was the people from the Old Farm. Shocked, Asia searched the top of the newspaper for a date. June 23, 1915.

Asia had memorized the date on the old auction poster in the museum. June 29, 1915. The man had drowned at the bridge just a few days before Miranda and George Williams decided to leave Cold Creek. Maddy knew. She had sensed the danger and nailed a horseshoe on one of the logs.

Asia's head reeled. She didn't understand what was happening. Who *was* Mary Wintergreen? Why did she have this old photograph and newspaper clipping in her house?

A feeling of dread swept through her. Her hands shaking, she slid the newspaper behind the brown paper and hung the photograph back on the wall. She was dimly aware of Sierra peering over her shoulder. "Oh look! That cat in the picture looks like Monty!"

Asia stepped backward. "We have to go! Right now!"

Sierra's eyes widened. Asia urged her through the door. The flickering flame of the oil lamp had gone out, and the hall was dark. It felt like the cottage was holding its breath. Her heart hammered wildly as they had made their way down the gloomy hall and back outside. She blinked in the bright sun. A seagull screeched, and the tangy smell of salt and seaweed stung her nose. She took a few deep breaths to steady herself.

"Aren't we going to say good-bye?" whispered Sierra.

"No." Asia took Sierra's hand and half ran to the front of the cottage. Her shoulders sagged with relief. Their bikes were still there. She glanced back at the cottage, her eyes pulled to the little round window high up in the thick vines. A face appeared, thin and pale, and she realized that it was Mary Wintergreen, watching them.

Sierra wheeled her bike ahead of Asia through the blue door. "We aren't coming back, are we?" she said.

Asia took one last look at the window. Mary Wintergreen was gone. "I don't know," she said slowly. As she followed Sierra out to the sidewalk, the faint notes of a piano drifted from within the old cottage.

CHAPTER THIRTY-TWO

Sierra lived in a green house with white shutters two streets below Beth. When they went inside Asia thought for a minute that Valerie was getting ready to move. She was standing on a kitchen chair, sweeping crumbs from an empty cupboard into a dustpan. The counters around her were buried in stacks of soup and fruit-cocktail cans, cereal and cracker boxes, a leaking bag of sugar, and bottles of soya sauce and salad dressing.

She pushed her hair back off her face and smiled weakly. "Spring cleaning...though I guess it's closer to fall. The mess just seems to build up. You look like you're feeling a lot better, Asia."

"I am," said Asia. She looked at the clutter of pictures and notices stuck on the fridge door: photographs of Sierra and Ben, a recipe torn from a magazine, a handprint with

Ben's name printed under it in big uneven letters, a green paper that had *Sam's Squash Schedule* scrawled across the top. Embarrassed, she glanced away quickly.

Ben raced into the room. He skidded to a stop and stared at Asia shyly. He was still in his pajamas and his hair stood up in all directions. "Hi," he said at last.

"Hi yourself," said Asia.

Valerie sighed and stepped off the chair. "We're having a bit of trouble getting going today. Will you stay for some lemonade?"

Asia longed to be alone so she could think about what had happened at Cormorant Cottage. "No thank you," she said. Ben's face fell, and she added, "Beth is probably wondering where I am."

She pushed her bike the last two blocks, her legs aching with sudden weariness, and let herself in the front door. A faint smell of cigarette smoke hung in the hall. She stood still for a moment, frowning. Beth called from the kitchen door, "Come in, Asia. There's someone here I want you to meet."

The woman sitting at the kitchen table was a stranger. She looked as old as Beth, but she was much heavier. She was wearing lots of makeup, and her hair was very blond. She put her cigarette on the rim of a saucer and stared at Asia. "Well, look at you. You turned out to be the spitting image of your mother."

"This is Gina Greenway, Asia," said Beth. "I told you we spoke the other day. She looked after you when you were a little girl."

"Hello," mumbled Asia.

"You don't remember me," said Gina. She laughed and picked up her cigarette. "It was a long time ago, kiddo. We used to be great pals."

Asia's face froze. Beth set a plate of cookies on the table. "Why don't you make the tea, Asia? Gina can't stay long. Her son dropped her off while he does some errands."

Beth always made the tea, and Asia felt a rush of gratitude that her grandmother had given her something to do. She took as long as she could, matching teacups and saucers, filling a little jug with milk while Beth and Gina talked.

"You don't mind me smoking, do you?" said Gina. "Sherri used to give me the dickens when I smoked in front of the baby." She laughed again, and for a second Asia thought she sounded nervous.

"I don't mind," said Beth, and Asia recognized the tiny tremor in her voice that meant she was trying not to smile. "Now please, go on."

Asia kept her eyes fixed on the kettle, her heart thudding against her ribs. Gina's voice was raspy and unfamiliar, and she told herself that this must be a mistake, that she had never seen this woman before in her whole life. But Gina was right into her story now, with only the occasional murmur from Beth, and Asia found herself unwillingly riveted to every word.

"Asia was two months old when Sherri and Tyler moved into the trailer next to ours. I said to my husband, they're just two babies themselves. Sherri didn't look more than sixteen. Tyler was older and of course I thought he was

Asia's daddy at first, but after they'd been there awhile Sherri told me he wasn't."

There was a short silence, as if Gina expected Beth to say something, then she sighed and said, "Tyler's sister met Sherri at a bus station and brought her home. They became friends and that's how she got to know Tyler. They seemed to be managing pretty good at first. I took extra blankets and some old baby clothes and the odd meal over to them, and Sherri had the trailer fixed up all nice and pretty. Tyler had a job with a moving company, and Sherri did some waitressing once she got on her feet again. I used to keep Asia over at my place when they were both working."

The kettle hissed, and Asia pulled out the plug and filled the teapot. She couldn't think of anything else she could do, so she carried the tea things to the table.

Gina beamed at her and her double chin wobbled. "Who'd have thought I'd be sitting having tea with my baby all grown up. That's what I used to call you—my baby. It drove Sherri crazy."

The blood rushed to Asia's cheeks. She busied herself stirring sugar lumps into her tea. She didn't like Gina. It was disgusting to eat cookies and smoke at the same time. She wondered meanly if she knew that her lipstick was wobbly.

"Then what happened?" said Beth quietly.

Gina took a long pull on her cigarette. "The problems started when Asia was about one and a half. Tyler was keen on being a daddy at first, but it wore off." She glanced at Asia. "It wasn't that he didn't like you. Everyone did. You were a cute kid." She wiped cookie crumbs from her chin.

"Tyler started putting a lot of pressure on Sherri to go out on weekends. My husband said you could hardly blame him—who'd want to be tied down at that age—but I told him you should think of things like that before you get involved with someone with a kid. I said babies aren't parcels to be passed around."

She paused expectantly, and Beth murmured in agreement. She caught Asia's eye and smiled.

"Anyway," said Gina, "they started going out a few Friday nights at first, and then Saturdays, and then before you knew it, it was every weekend. They'd drop Asia off at my trailer, and I'd end up keeping her until the morning. And then one day, Tyler left. It was a bit of a shock, though I did tell Sherri she was better off without him."

Gina helped herself to more tea and the last cookie, and Asia noticed with relief that Beth made no move to refill the plate.

"Sherri only stayed another six months or so. She said she couldn't pay the rent, but if you ask me, I think she was getting bored. She talked a lot about some commune in B.C. So Sherri bought herself an old truck and headed west. She promised to keep in touch, but she never did."

The silence lasted for a few minutes, and then a horn beeped outside. "That'll be my son," said Gina. She heaved herself out of her chair. "He hates waiting so I better get going. Good-bye, Asia. It's been a treat seeing you again, and I'm real sorry about your mom."

"Good-bye," mumbled Asia.

She waited until Beth had followed Gina to the front door.

Beth was saying something in a pleasant voice, but Asia wondered if inside she was upset. Gina hadn't made Sherri sound like a very good mother. Asia finished her tea at the window, watching Gina climb into a small brown car.

"She's on her way," said Beth, coming back into the kitchen.

Asia didn't look at Beth. "Now what happens?"

"Nothing happens."

"Aren't you going to ask her back?"

"I wasn't planning on it." Beth opened the fridge and took out a bag of broccoli and two carrots.

Asia tried to hide the relief that flooded through her.

"Gina is what my mother used to call a diamond in the rough." Beth picked up a knife and cut off a handful of broccoli spears. "She means well, and I'm sure she was very kind to you. And she's filled in a few gaps. But we don't have to be her new best friends."

Asia slid a teaspoon back and forth across the table-cloth. Pieces of her mother's life were still missing. Maybe Beth would try to find Tyler or Tyler's sister. They might even have seen Beth's notice and just hadn't got around to phoning yet. "Are you going to put any more notices in the paper?"

Beth put the broccoli down. "Do you think I should?"

"Not right now." Asia twirled the spoon, her shoulders tense.

"I agree," said Beth. "One Gina is enough."

Asia held back a smile. She stood up. "Is it okay if I read until supper?"

Beth didn't hear her. She had turned on the tap and was scrubbing the carrots. She looked tired, and there were lines on her face that Asia had never noticed before. She stood still for a minute, watching her grandmother. She was surprised to find herself wondering what it would have been like if Beth and not Gina had looked after her when she was little. She left the kitchen before she could give in to the urge to tell her grandmother about Mary Wintergreen and Cormorant Cottage.

CHAPTER THIRTY-THREE

After supper, Beth suggested they go out.

"Where would we go?" said Asia.

"The cemetery. I'd like you to see where Sherri is buried, and I want to take some fresh flowers."

Beth sent Asia into the garden with instructions to pick two bouquets of "anything pretty," one for Sherri and one for her grandfather, while Beth cleared up the supper things. Asia picked two big purple and pink bouquets and held them carefully on her lap in the car. The driveway into the cemetery wound between tall stately trees. A few cars passed them, going in the other direction, and Beth said, "This is my favorite time to come. Right before it closes. If we're lucky, we'll have the place to ourselves."

The parking lot was empty. Asia climbed out of the car and gazed around curiously. She had never been to a cemetery before, and she half expected to see bats swooping through the air and mist swirling around tombstones. But it was not like that at all. Long soft shadows fell across sweeping green lawns, crisscrossed by tidy gravel paths. Flat gravestones lay in neat rows, with bouquets of flowers dotting the ground with tiny splashes of color.

"Sherri and Ward are buried in the new part—just over there," said Beth.

Asia followed Beth along one of the paths, reading the inscriptions on the stones. Beth finally stopped in front of a flat gravestone surrounded by grass. "Here we are."

The blue flowers in the little pot at the top of Sherri's grave were faded, but they still looked pretty. Her grandmother must come here all the time, thought Asia in surprise.

She stared at the words on the gravestone. *Sherri Alexis Cumfrey 1976-1997. Our precious angel rests in peace.* Sherri had been an angel too, just like she was. She decided she didn't feel sad—just kind of hollow.

"How about putting some water in this container for me?" said Beth. "The tap's just over there by that tree."

Asia liked having something to do. She read more gravestones on the way there and back, and sat on a bench and watched her grandmother arrange the new flowers.

When she was finished, Beth perched beside her. "That looks better, doesn't it? You chose well, Asia. Sherri loved purple asters." Her voice was steady. "You must think we were terrible parents. But we had a lot of wonderful times with Sherri."

The blood rushed to Asia's cheeks. She swallowed hard.

"What happened?" she said.

Beth considered Asia's question. "A lot of things happened and nothing happened," she said finally. "That sounds silly, but that's how it seemed. Sherri was going through the usual teen stuff, no different than any of my friends' teenage daughters. Rebelling a little, wanting to stay out all night. It was hardest on Val. She was three years younger and worshiped Sherri. It hurt her when her sister ignored her."

"Anna used to play with Katya and me all the time," said Asia. "But now she goes in her bedroom and shuts the door, and she gets mad at Katya over nothing."

"Exactly," said Beth. "That's how it was with Sherri at first. Ward was very strict with her—too strict. They started having terrible fights. I used to take Valerie for a walk so she wouldn't have to listen to them yelling. Sherri thought everyone was against her and then, when she was sixteen, things started to go really wrong. Her marks dropped until she was failing, and she became so secretive. We were losing her, we knew that, but she wouldn't talk to any of us, not even Valerie. I was frantic. I knew she was holding something back from us, some huge secret. I even suspected drugs."

"Did you ever find out what it was?" said Asia. "Her secret?"

"Yes I did." Beth smiled gently. "As soon as Harry called, I figured it out. It was you, Asia. You were Sherri's secret. She ran away just over twelve years ago. She was pregnant with you."

Asia's heart thudded. Beth's voice sounded far away. "She sent one letter from Alberta to tell us that she was safe and that was the last we heard. I used to tell myself that she didn't hate us, that one day we would have our daughter back, but I was never sure. Your grandfather blamed himself for driving her away." She hesitated. "After we talked to the police, he convinced himself that she had been on her way home. It helped a little."

Maddy had wondered for all those years, and now she too believed that Sherri had been coming home. A different home. Cold Creek. Asia's heart filled with a sudden ache. She looked at Beth's smooth brown hands resting quietly on her lap, and wondered how she always stayed so calm.

"That last year, we didn't know any of Sherri's friends," said Beth. She paused. "So I've no idea who your father is."

Shocked, Asia examined what Beth had just said. She hadn't sounded like she was criticizing Sherri. She had just sounded kind of matter of fact. Asia leaned over and pulled out a blade of grass and studied it. "Are you going to try to find out?"

"Do you want me to?"

Asia shook her head. "Can we wait until later?"

"Of course."

They sat in silence for a few minutes and then Beth said, "Sherri was so like Ward. She kept everything inside and only let the anger out. I know I would have understood if she had talked to me about her problems." Beth reached out and touched Asia's arm gently. "I can understand why you might blame her."

Asia let the blade of grass fall between her knees. "Most of the time I don't know what I think," she said honestly.

Then she frowned. "Sierra blames Valerie, and I don't really get it because Sam is the one who left."

"Mmm," said Beth. "That one's complicated."

"Will Sam come back?"

"I don't know. But some time apart is not a bad idea. There's been way too much arguing in the house, and it upsets Ben and Sierra terribly."

Asia tried to imagine a house full of fighting. She couldn't remember ever hearing Maddy and Ira raise their voices at each other. Even when Maddy called Ira a stubborn old mule, you could hear the love in her voice. "I like Sierra," she was surprised to hear herself say.

"Well, she likes you," said Beth. "I think you're going to be good for her. She hasn't had the easiest time. She struggles a lot at school, especially with her reading. And she bottles everything up too. It would be helpful if she had someone to talk to."

Asia flushed. Sierra had tried to talk to her about Sam, and she had pushed her away. "I don't want to talk to Maddy right now," she said.

"I know," said Beth. "But she's willing to wait."

"She knows?"

"Of course she knows. She hasn't raised you all these years without figuring a few things out." Beth reached over and squeezed her hand. "You'll understand better one day when you're a mother."

Asia pulled her hand away. "I'm never going to be a mother. It's too hard."

Beth laughed. She stood up. "Let's go and put the flowers

on your grandfather's grave. And then do you want to go out somewhere for an ice-cream sundae?"

Asia loved ice-cream sundaes, but she couldn't ever remember feeling so tired. "I think I'd rather go home," she said softly.

CHAPTER THIRTY-FOUR

Asia woke up suddenly. The light outside her window was gray, and it took her a few seconds to remember where she was.

She slipped out of bed and padded downstairs in her bare feet. On the way to the kitchen, she glanced at the grandfather clock in the hall. It was not quite five-thirty, but she knew she would never be able to get back to sleep. A steady *tap tap tap* came through the open door of Beth's computer room. Her grandmother was working already, and Asia wondered curiously if she was always up this early.

She went into the kitchen and heated a pot of milk on the stove. She stirred in cocoa powder and sugar and, when it was warm, she poured some into a mug. She had made way too much. She hesitated and then filled another mug and carried it down the hall. She stood in the doorway of Beth's room and knocked.

"Come in." Beth didn't seem at all surprised to see Asia up so early. A delighted smile spread across her face. "You must have read my mind! Are you having some too?"

"Mine's in the kitchen," said Asia.

"Bring it in here," said Beth. "I should be embarrassed to invite you in because you'll see the dreadful mess I work in, but I could do with a little company."

Her grandmother didn't know that she had been in her room once before, thought Asia uncomfortably. When she got back, Beth had cleared the papers and magazines off a chair. "You're timing is perfect. I was starting to tear my hair out over this chapter."

Asia sat down. "Is the book going well?" she said, trying to sound polite.

Beth sighed. "Let's just say it's going. My problem is, I really prefer the research to the writing. I could pour over these old stories for ever."

Ghost stories, thought Asia. Her grandmother was researching ghost stories. But she wasn't supposed to know that. She longed suddenly to tell Beth about the ghost at the Old Farm, but then her grandmother would realize that she had been snooping through her papers. She sipped her cocoa and the warmth filled her. "What is your book about?" she said nervously.

"Ghosts." Beth tilted her chair back and stretched her long legs in front of her. "I've always been intrigued by ghost stories. Ever since I was little. Your great-grandmother

Minnie, my mother, claimed to have talked to all kinds of ghosts. Most people didn't believe her, but I did."

Asia took a big breath. "I would have believed her."

Her voice had sounded too loud. She pretended to be interested in her cocoa. Her grandmother's appraising gaze burned into the top of her head. "A lot of my research focuses on ghost sightings within families," said Beth. "I've read enough cases to suspect that there may be a genetic link." She paused. "That means that when one person in a family has the ability to see a ghost, you will often find others that can too."

Asia's hands were icy cold. She wrapped them around her cocoa mug. "I've seen a ghost," she whispered. "She lives at the Old Farm at Cold Creek. I've seen her twice."

She didn't dare look up. The silence in the room was complete. She sipped her cocoa nervously and then finally looked at her grandmother.

She could tell right away that Beth believed her. She was staring at Asia with both surprise and excitement in her eyes. "Tell me," she said.

The words spilled out of Asia. Beth listened attentively, popping in an occasional question, while Asia told her about sensing the ghost's presence at Dandy's grave, about the little pink bedroom with the bed that said *Daisy* and how the woman in the long blue dress had beckoned to her from the stairs. Not once did Beth look skeptical, not even when Asia described how she had seen the woman on the bridge in the middle of the night, and how she had heard that terrible cry.

"It's a fascinating story," said Beth at the end. "Were you ever frightened?"

"No," said Asia. "Well, maybe a tiny bit."

"She sounds so mysterious," said Beth, "and I think very sad. I wonder who she is?"

"I think her name is Miranda Williams," said Asia. "It's the name on an old auction poster at the museum. It says people called George and Miranda Williams used to live at the Old Farm at Cold Creek."

"I wish that I had made the time to go and see the Old Farm while I was there," said Beth.

"I think Daisy must have been their daughter," said Asia.

"That makes sense."

"The lady at the museum said they probably left Cold Creek because of the war. But Maddy always had a feeling it was something else."

"And I think we can trust Maddy's hunches," said Beth. "It's intriguing, isn't it? Whatever could have happened? And I wonder why it's Miranda and not George who's haunting Cold Creek?"

It was just like a mystery novel, only this was real. "Can anyone else in my family see ghosts?" said Asia. "Can you?"

"No, but I wish I could," said Beth. "I think your great-great-aunt might have communicated with ghosts. My mother's sister Jane. She died of a mysterious illness when she was just about your age. But I have a few old family letters that describe her as quite fanciful. A storyteller with too much imagination, one letter says. But I think Jane was telling stories about ghosts."

"I think so too," said Asia quickly. "Jane is my middle name. Do you think that's just a coincidence?"

"No, I don't," said Beth firmly. "Sherri was always fascinated by the story of her great aunt. Apparently Jane spent most of her life confined to bed, and the doctors were never able to find a cure. She died when she was ten or eleven. Sherri thought it was so tragic."

It *was* tragic, thought Asia instantly. Her imagination floated around a dark cold room lit by candles and a little girl's pale face and haunted eyes. A thrill ran through her.

"If you like, I'll dig out the letters for you."

"Yes please," said Asia quickly.

A great-grandmother called Minnie and a great-great-aunt called Jane who had talked to ghosts. And now her. Asia's head whirled. "Why me?" she said. "Why can I see ghosts?"

"I'm not sure," said Beth. "But I do know from my research that it runs in families and can skip a generation or two."

They sat in silence for a few minutes. Beth smiled at Asia. "You're falling asleep in your chair, and I've got a little bit of work here to finish."

"No I'm not," said Asia as she tried to swallow a huge yawn.

Beth laughed. "Scoot back to bed for a couple of hours, and we'll talk later. You've given me a lot to think about, Asia Cumfrey."

Bed did sound tempting. Asia paused in the doorway. "Why *do* ghosts haunt old places?"

"Well," said Beth, "a lot of ghosts are trapped on earth because of a violent death or a tragedy. They're being punished, and they need someone or something to set them free before they can leave the world of the living.

Asia dragged her feet upstairs, her thoughts in a muddle. Something violent and tragic had happened at the bridge. A man had drowned. But she couldn't tell Beth about the faded newspaper clipping hidden behind the old photograph of Daisy. Not yet. Her grandmother might tell her she couldn't go back to Cormorant Cottage. And she had to go back, just one more time.

CHAPTER THIRTY-FIVE

The rain started after Asia went back to bed, and kept up a steady downpour until early afternoon. Beth found the old family letters about Jane, and Asia pored through them, fascinated.

I am worried about little Jane, wrote someone called Aunt Dorothy. *She tells such tales about a child who comes into her room at night and talks to her. It is one thing to have an imagination but really, she is taking it too far...*

Jane *had* been seeing ghosts, Asia was sure of it. "We're an interesting family, anyway," said Beth when she checked on Asia, and Asia agreed.

Finally the sky started to clear. Asia stuffed a waterproof poncho of Beth's into her backpack and headed straight to Cormorant Cottage. She pushed away her guilt at not stopping to pick up Sierra. This was something she had to do by herself.

Mary Wintergreen greeted her at the door, her cold hand gripping Asia's tightly.

"Maybe I should look in the other rooms today," said Asia hopefully. "The kitchen or the bathroom." After all, Montgomery could have dropped her medal anywhere in the cottage.

"Oh no," said Mary Wintergreen, staring at Asia with her penetrating gaze. "If the diary were in there, I would have found it myself," she added. "But keep looking. I'll make tea after I've had a rest."

So Asia climbed the attic stairs and spent an hour searching listlessly for the diary. She found nothing. She peeked out the little window. Water dripped from the gloomy trees, and the vines glistened with raindrops. It was drizzling again. Monty stalked through the long grass, shaking the water off his paws with each step. Asia leaned out the window and watched him until he disappeared into the thick shrubbery below her. Music sounded faintly in the distance, and she pulled herself in and walked across the dusty floor to the top of the stairs. She peered into the darkness. The music was coming from inside the cottage. Mary Wintergreen must be playing the piano in the parlor.

The cottage didn't seem scary today, just empty and lonely. There was no sign that anyone else ever came here. Asia had never even seen a telephone. She sighed. The missing diary might be an excuse to give the old woman some company. Maybe it didn't even exist. And her Saint Christopher medal seemed to have vanished forever. She picked up her backpack and tiptoed downstairs. She was going to tell Mary Wintergreen that she was going home, that she didn't want the job anymore. But first she wanted to have one more look at the photograph of Daisy.

The oil lamp flickered weakly in the dim hallway, and soft piano notes drifted through the closed parlor door. Asia quietly opened the door across from the attic stairs and slipped inside the old bedroom. A breeze blew across the room, and the faded flowered curtains moved gently over the window. The old pale green quilt on the bed was smooth and unwrinkled. Asia had a feeling the old woman wasn't using the room; it had such an air of emptiness about it. But she must have come in here to open the window, maybe to air it out.

She put her backpack on the floor and studied the photograph of Daisy. The little girl's narrow lively face made her think of an elf. Her imagination stirred. It was easy to picture Daisy playing in the pink bedroom in the house at the Old Farm, her tiny feet clattering up and down the stairs. She must be dead now, or else very very old. Had she and Mary Wintergreen known each other? Had they been friends? Is that why the picture was here? Asia frowned. Why a picture of Daisy when she was a little girl? And who had hidden the old newspaper clipping about the man who had drowned at the bridge?

A sudden movement from the corner of the room made her heart jump. She spun around. Monty's slanted gold eyes stared at her from the shadows on top of the wardrobe. "You like it up there, don't you?" she said.

Monty pushed something with his paw across the top of the wardrobe. Asia walked over to the wardrobe and reached up her hand. She slid it back and forth, and her fingers closed on something smooth and hard.

Her Saint Christopher medal.

"Thank you," she breathed. "Thank you so much." She slipped the chain over her neck. Monty's tail lashed back and forth. She had the odd sensation again that the cat was looking right inside her brain. His eyes were steady and unblinking. He gave a few sharp mews.

"There's something else, isn't there?" whispered Asia. "What are you trying to tell me?"

The glass on the mirror on the front of the wardrobe was ripply, and the reflection of her face was pale and wavy. She pulled the little glass handle on the door. She wiggled it back and forth and the door swung open.

The faint scent of lavender drifted over her. Long dresses hung on hangers, and the top shelf was filled with folded quilts. Monty jumped to the floor and rubbed up against her legs, meowing loudly. She stood on her tiptoes and slid her hand behind the quilts. Her fingers bumped against something hard. She pulled it out. It was a small box made of pale creamy yellow wood with a delicate carved butterfly on the lid. She recognized it right away. It was one of Ira's boxes.

CHAPTER THIRTY=SIX

The box was part of Ira's butterfly collection, the very first set of boxes he had made when he and Maddy came to Cold Creek almost fifty years ago. Maddy had kept two in the house, and she said she would never sell them. But Ira had sold the rest. He told Asia proudly how even in those days people drove all the way to Cold Creek to buy one of his butterfly boxes.

Asia sat on the edge of the bed, stunned. How had Ira's box got to Cormorant Cottage? She lifted the lid. After all this time, it slipped off easily. The box was empty. She examined the lid for a second and then carefully pressed one of the butterfly's wings. The pale yellow wood on the bottom of the lid slid back. Tucked in a narrow compartment underneath was a slim brown leather book.

Her heart racing, she picked it up. The leather was soft and worn. She opened the cover and read the words in sloping black letters on the first page. *The Diary of Miranda Williams.*

Stunned, Asia stared at the book. Nothing made any sense. Daisy's picture, Ira's box and now Miranda's diary. Why were they here in Cormorant Cottage? And who *was* Mary Wintergreen? She turned over a few pages. They were covered with more of the beautiful handwriting, line after line, the words small and close together. She read some of the dates. *December 4, 1914. February 10, 1915. April 8, 1915.* The diary was almost a hundred years old.

A piece of stiff paper stuck out between the pages near the end of the book, almost like a marker, and she opened it to that spot. A small square photograph, the edges yellowed with age, was tucked into the crease of the book. It was of a little girl standing on the porch of the house at the Old Farm. Thick curly hair framed her round plump cheeks. Asia turned it over. There was writing on the back, the same sloping black handwriting as the diary. *Daisy at Cold Creek, 1914.*

For a second, she thought she had made a mistake. She looked up and stared at the tiny elfin face in the oval frame above the washstand. Then she walked across the room, lifted the picture off the wall and turned it over.

Daisy, 1915. The letters sloped across the back of the photograph—there was no question about that—but it couldn't be right. The little girls in the two pictures were not the same person. So that meant there had been *two* girls called Daisy at the Old Farm at Cold Creek. Someone had taken their pictures one year apart, and Miranda had written *Daisy* on the back of each photograph in her distinctive handwriting. Asia hung the photograph back on the wall and lowered herself onto the bed. An odd hush had settled over the room, and the soft haunting notes of the piano sounded far away. She picked up the little book, still open at the place marked by the photograph.

> *May 18, 1915*
> *Today a stranger came to Cold Creek. He rode out of the mountains mounted on a big black stallion and leading a packhorse. Our farm is remote, but we have had visitors before. I don't know why I feel this sense of foreboding.*

The slanted handwriting became harder to read as Asia turned the pages—the letters jerky and uneven, as if the writer were ill. She had written pages and pages about Beatrice, recording in painstaking detail the new words she learned each day, the clothes she had dressed her in, the games they had played, a trip to a hotel when she had pretended Beatrice was Daisy. Asia shivered. There must have been something very wrong with Miranda. She flipped ahead. There was only one more entry, and then the writing stopped, and the rest of the book was blank. She strained to decipher the cramped words of the last entry.

> *June 21, 1915*
> *It has taken me three days to write this.*
> *My hand is shaking and I fear my letters are badly*

formed, but I will do my utmost to record everything that happened three days ago.

By dusk, the rain that had plagued us for days stopped. I left Beatrice in George's care and went for a walk in the fresh air. I walked much farther than I intended, following the swollen creek. It was getting dark when I reached the bridge.

I saw the log that George had put at one end to warn Blackmore not to cross. I shuddered when I looked at the icy water that raged below. A man might be able to walk across the bridge, George had said. But it would never take the weight of horses.

A cool breeze washed over my arms, and a thin sliver of moon broke through the clouds. I don't know how long I stood there.

The log was heavier than I expected.

I rolled it off the bridge. The raging water grabbed it and carried it away. I have no memory of leaving the bridge, but I must have done so. A long while later, a black horse and rider, leading a second horse, emerged from the forest on the other side of the creek. It was of course Blackmore. His stallion strode over the trail quickly, and he was almost at the bridge. He didn't notice me standing in the grove of dark trees.

A voice inside my head urged me to warn him. My throat was dry and my heart hammered against my chest.

I was silent. For a second, everything stood still. It was not too late but still I did nothing. I had the odd sensation that I was looking at a picture, that none of this was real. Then the horses stepped onto the bridge, snorting at the black water foaming below. They were halfway across when the bridge gave way with a groan and a sharp cracking sound. Blackmore cursed and a horse screamed. In a few seconds, the bridge collapsed, and the horses and rider were swept down the raging creek. I stared at the water and remembered Blackmore telling George that he could not swim a stroke.

A strange calmness fell over me as I walked across the dark meadow to our farm. When the lights of our house appeared in the distance, my steps quickened.

Daisy was waiting for me. She had found a treasure. It was hidden inside her tiny hands. "Come see!" she cried. She opened her fingers. A pale shadow fluttered in her palm. It rose into the air and escaped to the window, beating its wings against the black glass.

It was a white moth.

Asia dropped the diary in her lap. The piano music had stopped and the cottage was silent. She stared at the narrow elfin face in the photograph over the washstand. The date on the back said 1915. One year after Daisy had died. "Beatrice," she whispered. "You're Beatrice Blackmore."

Now she knew why Miranda Williams was doomed to haunt the Old Farm. Miranda had killed Beatrice's father, Ridley Blackmore, and then she had turned Beatrice into Daisy.

CHAPTER THIRTY=SEVEN

"Hello!" called a man's voice. "Is anyone in here? Hello!" Asia froze and stared at the bedroom door. Heavy footsteps sounded on floorboards. "Is anyone here?"

The footsteps stopped. Asia stood up. Her heart hammering, she slipped Ira's box and the diary into her backpack and slung the pack over her shoulders. The curtains at the window swished and there was a thump as Monty jumped over the sill onto the ground. Inside the cottage, a door banged. Asia crossed the room and opened the bedroom door, blinking in the sudden bright light. A glass light fixture hung from the ceiling halfway down the hall, and at the far end a man in a brown jacket and jeans stared at her with an irritated look on his face. "Is that your bike out there? Do you realize you're trespassing, young lady?"

Asia's throat was dry. "I'm not trespassing," she stammered. "I'm helping Mary Wintergreen." She stared around wildly. What had happened to the hall? It was so brightly lit. The oil lamp was gone and instead of the dingy mauve wallpaper, the walls were painted a creamy yellow.

The man gave her a long hard look. Then he said, "Come on, let's go. You've no business breaking into empty houses. There's nothing in here to take anyway. I've a good mind to let your parents know what you've been doing."

Asia felt dizzy. It was hard to breathe. From far away she heard the man say, "Hurry now. I have no idea how you got in here, but I want to lock everything up."

She stumbled down the hall. Panic swept over her as she glanced through the open parlor door. The room was empty, the piano and chairs and books gone, the crimson curtains removed and the dark trees outside visible through the bare windows. A few dust balls clung to the corners, and an empty cardboard box lay on its side in the middle of the floor.

The man moved to the side and waited while she slid past him, and then he switched off the light and followed her outside to the porch. The sagging armchair and the rocking chair had vanished, and a few dried leaves were scattered across the steps. Asia's head spun and she thought she was going to be sick. "I don't understand," she whispered. "What happened to the cottage? Where's Mary Wintergreen?"

The man's eyes softened slightly. "You look as white as a sheet. Look, maybe you've just made an honest mistake. There's no one here by the name of Mary Wintergreen. This cottage belongs to Miss Williams. We live next door and we're keeping an eye on it for her."

Asia stared at the man. "What do you mean? Who's Miss Williams?"

The man turned a key in the lock and rattled the door a few times. "I just told you. She owns this cottage. She's living at the Oceanview Rest Home on Marine Drive now. She's very elderly, and the cottage is too much for her. I'm waiting to hear what she's decided to do with it."

"She can't own this cottage," said Asia weakly. "Mary Wintergreen does."

The man's eyes hardened again. "I don't know if you're trying to be funny, but I don't have time for it. And I'm still not sure how you got in. That door in the fence is supposed to be locked too. I've got better things to do than chase kids out of this house, so off you go now."

Asia stumbled around the side of the cottage. As she reached for her bike, cool air brushed against her arm. "Please," said a voice. "Listen carefully. Please, it's very important."

It was Mary Wintergreen's voice.

"Please..."

Asia's disbelief turned quickly to shock. Mary Wintergreen must be a ghost. It was the only way to make sense of everything. She gazed around wildly. "Where are you?" she said. "What do you want?"

"You must take her the diary..." The voice was much fainter now, and Asia had trouble hearing the words. "Please...the rest home...she must be told."

"Go on!" yelled the man suddenly. He was standing at the side of the cottage, watching her. "Miss Williams doesn't want kids hanging around here."

"I *am* going!" said Asia.

You must take her the diary.

Miss Williams? Was that who Mary Wintergreen was talking about? Did she want Asia to take the diary to Miss Williams at the rest home?

Asia hesitated, straining to hear the voice again, but she was surrounded by silence. She picked up her bike and wheeled it out to the street.

~

The Oceanview Rest Home was a big sea-blue building surrounded by shrubs and flower beds. Asia chained her bike to a sign near the front entrance and walked up to the glass doors. She hesitated and then pressed a silver button. A voice muffled by static said, "Yes?" Asia took a big breath. "I've come to see Miss Williams."

There was a long buzzing sound. Asia pushed the door open and went inside. A row of wrinkled faces stared at her from their wheelchairs in the front lobby. "Hello dear," said an old lady in a pink housecoat.

Asia smiled nervously. A woman wearing a yellow smock and a nametag that said *Sarah* came out from behind the reception desk. "Hello! You haven't been here before, have you? I'll show you to Miss Williams' room. This will be a real treat. She doesn't get many visitors."

Asia followed Sarah down a long hallway, past a man with a walker and a nurse pushing a woman in a wheelchair.

"Everyone's starting to head down for supper," explained Sarah, "but you've got a little time."

She paused outside a partly open door, tapped gently and then pushed it wide open. "You're awake, I see. Look what I've brought you."

She crossed the room and straightened a pink crocheted afghan on the knees of the small, wrinkled, white-haired woman in the armchair by the window. "Isn't this a nice surprise? You have a visitor, Daisy."

CHAPTER THIRTY-EIGHT

Sarah left, and Asia hesitated in the doorway, feeling suddenly nervous.

"Asia. What a pretty name," the old woman said. "Come in and perch on my bed. If you dig in that top drawer, you'll find a tin of biscuits."

"I'm not hungry, thank you." Asia put her backpack on the floor and sat on the pale yellow bedspread. The room was small and very warm, and cluttered with books and knickknacks. The tiny old woman was watching her with keen bird-like eyes, her hands folded neatly on the afghan.

She doesn't know, thought Asia. She doesn't know that her real name is Beatrice Blackmore. She looked away and her eyes rested on a faded photograph in a square frame on the night table. She stared at it, shocked. It was a photograph of Mary Wintergreen in her rocking chair on the porch of the Cormorant Cottage. The big gray cat lay asleep in her lap.

"My mother," said Daisy, watching Asia carefully. "It was taken just about a year before she died."

Asia's body went rigid. "What was her name?"

"Miranda Williams."

Disbelief and then fear swept through Asia.

Daisy smiled. "I'm what you call an old maid. I never married. My mother and I lived together until she died."

"In Cormorant Cottage," whispered Asia. Her head reeled. Mary Wintergreen was really Miranda Williams.

Curiosity flickered in the old lady's eyes. "Yes, it was my childhood home. We moved there from the Cariboo when I was four. My father was killed the next year in the war, and my mother and I stayed on in the cottage. She died forty years ago, and by then I couldn't imagine living anywhere else. You'll think this is funny, but I used to feel that she was still with me. I imagined that I could hear her making tea. I made a few changes to the cottage to brighten it up, but mostly I kept it the same."

Asia's heart raced. She undid her backpack and slid out the butterfly box. "Ahh," said Daisy. She leaned forward with interest. "You've been to my cottage, I see. I thought that box had disappeared years ago. Wherever did you find it?"

"It was in an old wardrobe," said Asia. "Monty helped me." She paused, her face burning. The old lady would have no idea what she was talking about. How could Asia explain what she was doing in her cottage? How could she tell her that she had talked to her dead mother?

But Daisy didn't seem surprised. "Mama's wardrobe. The last time I saw that it was in the corner of the attic, full of musty old clothes. I could never bear to go through it. It brought back too many memories. I put a lot of Mama's heavy old furniture in the attic after she died."

"It was in the bedroom—" Asia stopped. She had an eerie feeling that if she went back to the cottage, the bedroom would be as bare and empty as the parlor. She took a big breath. "How did you get this box?"

"Well now, that's something I haven't thought about for years." Daisy's eyes sparkled. "About ten years before my mother died, we went on a trip together. We drove way up into the Cariboo to a place called Cold Creek."

Asia stared at Daisy. "Was there anybody living there?"

"Oh yes. There was a lovely young couple in a big gray house. I remember the woman served us tea and scones."

Maddy and Ira. Asia's heart gave a jump.

"Mama said we had lived at Cold Creek too, when I was a little girl, and she wanted me to see it. She was so excited when she planned the trip, but when we got there she seemed uneasy."

"Did your mother tell the people who she was?" said Asia.

"No," said Daisy. "She insisted that we just pretend to be visitors. People in the nearby town had told us about the man's workshop. Mama said we could pretend to be buying a box. She told me that the big gray house wasn't the house where I had lived, and after the tea we went for a walk to an old abandoned farm. Mama was terribly upset when she saw it, and I remember suggesting that we leave. But she said that there was something that she had to show me." Daisy closed her eyes. She looked frail and exhausted, as if the effort of talking were too much, and she murmured, "My dear, are you really interested in the ramblings of an old woman? And who did you say you were?"

"My name is Asia. And I am interested. But I can come back if you like."

The old lady blinked slowly and gazed at the photograph on the night table. "No, no. It's odd. I don't always know what I had for breakfast but those long-ago days are very clear to me. I think I was going to tell you about the grave. A child's grave. There wasn't much there, just some old pieces of fence lying in the grass, but Mama said it was the right place."

"Did she tell you whose grave it was?" said Asia.

Daisy stared into the distance. "My sister," she said finally. "Her name was Daisy too. She died a year before I was born, and Mama named me after her."

Asia wondered if Miranda had meant to tell her the truth then, but had been too afraid. She frowned. She had explored all around the Old Farm, and she had never seen any sign of a grave. "Do you remember where the grave was?"

"I don't think we walked very far from the house," said Daisy. "Mama said she couldn't bear to think of my sister being alone. I think it was on a bank looking down on the creek." She sighed. "It was a long walk back across the meadows, and my mother was exhausted when we got to the house. She was almost eighty, after all. The woman was kind and invited us inside, but Mama said no. She waited in the car, but I insisted on seeing the man's workshop before we left."

She gestured at the butterfly box on Asia's knee. "It's lovely, isn't it? I was delighted with it, and I always loved the secret compartment."

"Did Miranda...did your mother know about it?" said Asia.

"No," said Daisy. "No, I'm sure she didn't. She knew I bought a box, and I may have told her about the compartment, but she wouldn't have paid much attention." She hesitated. "Mama never liked the box. She was upset by the trip, and I think it just brought back difficult memories."

There was a long silence. Asia swallowed. "I found your mother's diary," she said slowly. "It was in the secret compartment." She took a big breath. "Did you hide it there?"

Daisy blinked at Asia. "Hide her diary? Oh no, it wasn't me." Her wrinkled fingers twisted the edge of her afghan. "I knew my mother had a diary. She was always very secretive with it. When I was a child I sometimes saw her reading it. I was forbidden to touch it."

Daisy rummaged in a crackly paper bag on the table beside her and took out a peppermint wrapped in cellophane. "Here you are, dear."

"Thank you," said Asia, trying to hide her impatience.

Daisy nodded. "Now, we were talking about the diary, weren't we? How odd it should turn up now. I've always thought that my mother destroyed it years ago."

"But she didn't," said Asia. "And then someone hid it in the box. Who would have done that?"

Daisy's eyes fluttered, but her voice was still clear. "We had a girl living with us from France. Claudette. She was with us for a few months before Mama died, helping with the housework and keeping Mama company during the days when I was working. I was a schoolteacher you know, for forty-five years. Claudette's the only person besides me who knew about the secret compartment. I showed her how it worked, and she often played with it. She left shortly after Mama died, and the box disappeared then too. I always suspected Claudette took it back to France."

But she hadn't. Asia had a vivid picture of the French girl sliding the diary into the secret drawer and tucking the box behind the quilts in the old wardrobe.

"Claudette visited Mama in the hospital the night before she died," said Daisy slowly. "I think I know what might have happened. You see, Claudette's English was very poor, and Mama would have known she would never have been able to read the diary. She must have asked Claudette to hide it somewhere until she came home. And then Mama didn't come home. She died in the hospital."

Something flashed through Daisy's eyes—a memory that was painful and hard. She murmured, "Yes, I see it now...I was forbidden to ever touch the diary...It must have been Claudette..." She straightened and looked at Asia steadily. "And now you have brought the diary to me. You must be my neighbor's daughter. Your father is so kind..."

Asia took the little book out of her backpack and put it on the table beside Daisy's chair. "Your mother wants you to read it," she said. "She wants you to know her secret."

There was a tap at the door. It was Sarah. She smiled at Asia and then turned to Daisy. "It's time to take you down for supper, my dear."

"No," said Daisy wearily. "No, I'm going to skip supper tonight."

Sarah tilted her head, but her expression was kind. "I'll sneak you up some toast and apple juice later," she promised, and she shut the door quietly behind her.

"She's a lovely girl," said Daisy. "They are all so thoughtful here. I'm ninety-five you know. I'll stay here until the end now. I'm selling Cormorant Cottage."

Her hands trembled. "Now what were we talking about?"

"The diary," said Asia. "Your mother's secret."

"Oh, yes, the diary." Daisy's voice quavered and then she fell silent. Asia wished with a sudden fervor that she had never come, had never brought the diary with its terrible secret to this peaceful old lady.

When Daisy spoke next, her voice was clear and firm. "I'm afraid I don't see very well anymore. Certainly not well enough to read something like that. You keep it, my dear, and leave me the box. I was always so fond of that little box." Her eyes floated shut and she murmured, "And my memories, you must leave me my memories…"

Asia picked up the diary and her backpack and tiptoed to the door. When she looked back, Daisy was sleeping quietly, her hands resting softly on her pink afghan.

CHAPTER THIRTY-NINE

When Asia let herself into the house, Beth was out. She had left a message on the kitchen counter telling Asia to check the answering machine. She pressed the flashing button and listened to Sam's voice. *I'm taking Sierra on a secret mission tonight. Includes supper. I need Asia's help. I'll pick her up at six o'clock.*

Asia felt exhausted and would rather have crawled into bed so she could think about everything that had happened. She splashed cold water over her face and then waited for Sam's car in the driveway. Sierra waved excitedly out the window and hung over the back of the seat while Asia put on her seatbelt. "We're going to the White Spot for dinner! The drive-in! And Ben's not coming!"

When they got there Sierra debated for ten minutes over the Pirate Pak until Sam finally flicked on the headlights to signal that they were ready.

After Sam put in their order, he turned sideways to Sierra and said, "So, can you guess the surprise?"

Asia saw by his face that he realized his mistake instantly. But it was too late. "You're coming home," said Sierra.

Sam looked stricken. "I can't, pumpkin. Not right now."

Asia watched Sierra hold her eyes very wide for a minute. Then she pointed her chin in the air and said, "What is it then?"

Sam pretended he was holding a bugle. "Ta da da da da. You are getting your ears pierced tonight!"

Sierra screeched and gave Sam a huge bear hug. Sam grinned at Asia over Sierra's head. "Your mother has provided the earrings, and I'm taking you to the torture chamber. And I'm counting on Asia for advice and moral support. She's been through it."

Asia laughed. "Maddy pierced my ears with a darning needle."

"No way!" yelled Sierra, and Sam grimaced. "Sterilized, I hope."

"In a pot of boiling water on the woodstove," said Asia.

"Hmm," said Sam. "Sierra, if Asia survived that, I think you're going to be okay."

When the food arrived, it smelled delicious. Asia dug into her hamburger with a huge first bite. She was starving.

In a sudden panic Sierra mumbled through a mouthful of French fries, "You mustn't tell Grandma. I want it to be a secret. Promise?"

There had been too many secrets. But this one was fun.

"I promise," said Asia.

The earrings were a huge success. Beth got a quick peek when they dropped Asia off and was suitably impressed. Asia's eyelids felt like heavy weights, and she stumbled to bed right after they left. She had so much to tell Beth, but Valerie had called just as Sam and Sierra were leaving, and Asia knew that Beth would be ages.

She lay on her back, wide-awake, waiting for Beth to get off the phone. She went over and over in her mind all the things that had happened. When she had seen Miranda in the old house and that night on the bridge, she had known she was a ghost. But Mary Wintergreen had seemed like a real person. And why had she made up the name Mary Wintergreen anyway?

Miranda was trying to make contact with me at Cold Creek, thought Asia with a sudden shiver. She was certain now that it was Miranda that she had heard at Dandy's grave. And then Miranda had tried to talk to her in the old house, but Asia had run away. Asia rolled restlessly onto her side. In a way there were two ghosts. The ghost of the young Miranda at Cold Creek and the ghost of the old Miranda who had lived at Cormorant Cottage and who had told Asia she was Mary Wintergreen.

And what about George? Did he know what Miranda had done? The date on the auction poster at the museum was June 29, 1915. That fit with the dates in the diary. George and Miranda must have left Cold Creek soon after Ridley Blackmore drowned. Asia frowned, trying to think what Beatrice had said about her father. Then she remembered.

George had been killed in the war the year after he and Miranda had left Cold Creek.

Asia sat up. Her head whirled with so many questions. She had to talk to Beth. She slipped out of bed and went out into the hall. Her grandmother's calm voice drifted up the stairs, interspersed with long pauses. With a sigh, Asia went back to her room, crawled under the covers and went to sleep.

~

It felt like only a few minutes had passed when the shrill ring of the phone woke her. Two more rings...then silence. Asia snuggled deeper into her blankets and tried to go back to sleep. But it was too late. She was wide-awake. She rolled over with a groan. The room was gray with the dawn, and the clock on her dresser blinked 5:00 AM. Who would phone this early?

The door slid open, and Beth sat down beside her on the bed. "That was Harry," she said. "Oh Asia. It's not good news."

Ira. Asia stared at her grandmother.

"Ira died a few hours ago," said Beth softly. "The pneumonia caused complications. But Maddy said he wasn't suffering. He passed away peacefully in his sleep."

Asia felt Beth's arms around her as she struggled against the pain that exploded inside her chest. Her shoulders heaved with sobs. It was hard to breathe.

After a long time she whispered, "I need Maddy."

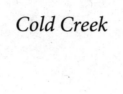

Cold Creek

CHAPTER FORTY

This time Miranda knew what brought her back to Cold Creek. It was time to say good-bye. She went for one last walk to Ira and Maddy's house, Montgomery bounding ahead through the meadow. The yard was full of cars and trucks, and people sat on chairs and blankets under the trees. Women went in and out of the house carrying trays of food and pitchers and glasses. Most of the people were strangers, but she recognized the tall gray-haired woman who had taken Asia away in the red car. Did that mean that Asia was back at Cold Creek too? The woman was talking to the man who reminded her of the little boy called Harry. It was like a party, she thought, only there was so much sadness in the air it almost choked her.

She was about to go back to the Old Farm when she spotted Asia sitting beside Maddy on the porch. She was crying.

What had happened to make her so sad? She wished that she could help her, but already she was fading. She knew she had only a little time left.

There was so much that she wanted to tell Asia, but it was too late. She remembered her excitement at the old dog's grave when she first realized that Asia had heard her speak. She smiled wistfully. She had been too impatient, she hadn't thought things through, and she had scared her away that day at the Old Farm.

Miranda's attention was drawn back to the house. People were moving to their trucks and cars. The gathering was breaking up. Montgomery rubbed against her skirt, and she reached down and picked him up. Precious Monty, always so faithful. She looked at Asia one last time. Her face was pressed against Maddy, who was softly stroking her long black hair. Miranda turned away and walked back to the Old Farm to finish tidying Daisy's grave.

⁓

Miranda cleared away the last of the ugly thistles. The grass was soft and golden over Daisy's grave. The wooden cross was in perfect shape, the lettering as freshly painted as when George made it almost a hundred years ago. *Daisy Sarah Williams 1911-1914. Rest in peace with God.* She walked down to the creek and picked a bouquet of late purple asters, and then carried them back to the grave and laid them at the foot of the cross.

She glanced up at Daisy's bedroom window. She had opened the window wide to let in the fresh air, and the pink curtains blew gently over the sill. She was ready to leave

Cold Creek for the last time. She sat on the grass beside the cross. There had been fog and frost in the morning, but now the sky was deep blue.

All of her senses were awakened as she waited on the bank above the creek. The water sparkled like blue jewels and the grass gleamed like gold. A meadowlark burst into song. The heat of the sun warmed her back for the first time in forty years. She looked at the neat wooden cross and the bouquet of purple asters, and a feeling of profound peace filled her heart. It was time to go. She only wished she had been able to thank Asia. She sat very still, and the suffering and pain of the last forty years floated away. She was free.

CHAPTER FORTY-ONE

The Celebration of Life for Ira was over, the last car disappearing around the bend in the road. Beth and Harry washed dishes in the kitchen and dealt with the mountains of food left by neighbors and friends. Asia sat with Maddy on the porch.

"Ira said that migrating birds always come back," said Asia.

"That's right," said Maddy, squeezing her hand. "The robins, the swallows, the red-winged blackbirds. And we'll come back to Cold Creek too. Next summer."

"Ira won't," whispered Asia.

Maddy was quiet for a minute. "I don't think Ira has gone," she said finally. "I think he's still here, in the places he loved so much."

"His workshop," said Asia.

"Oh yes," said Maddy. "And his favorite fishing holes."

"The meadows," said Asia. "He always walked in the meadows."

"The mountains," said Maddy. "He liked to sit with his coffee and look at the mountains."

Asia sat still for a few minutes, holding tightly to the idea of Ira all around them. "Will you like California?" she said after awhile.

"I think so," said Maddy. "I'll like spending time with Harry. But I'll miss you terribly."

Asia sighed. "Harry's okay."

Maddy smiled. "Yes, he is. And I've always been fond of Joyce. What about you? Will you be all right with Beth?"

"Yes," said Asia slowly. "There's Sierra too. Beth wants me to help her with her reading. And I like Valerie, and Ben is cute. And Sam is nice too, though Valerie is very mad at him right now."

"Families aren't always easy," said Maddy. "Now don't forget, I'm going to fly to Vancouver to spend Christmas with you and Beth. I'll get to meet everyone then."

The sun had dipped behind the trees, and the air was growing cooler. The screen door opened behind them, and Beth stepped onto the porch. "We've cleaned up enough for now," she said. "Do you think we have time to walk to the Old Farm before it gets dark? I want to see where it all began."

Asia had told Maddy and Beth the whole story of Miranda's ghost, Mary Wintergreen and Cormorant Cottage, and they had both read the small brown diary with fascination. Asia looked at Maddy. "Will you come?"

"I don't think so," said Maddy. "I'm a little tired, and I think I'll just sit." She smiled at Asia. "But you go. It won't be dark for an hour."

Asia hesitated. "Are you sure?'

"I'm sure."

Asia stood up. "We won't be too long," she said. "There's just one thing I need to know."

≈

Asia gazed at the bare walls and dusty floor in the house at the Old Farm. "I don't feel anything," she said. "I don't think Miranda is here."

"You set her free when you took the diary to Beatrice," said Beth. "It was Beatrice's choice what happened after that." She walked over to the window beside the front door and looked out. "I wonder how many times Miranda looked out at this very scene, checking the sky for storms, watching for George to come home. I can imagine the day Beatrice and Blackmore rode out of those mountains. It wouldn't have looked much different from today."

"I'm glad Beatrice didn't read the diary," said Asia. "I'm glad she didn't have to know."

"I am too," said Beth. "I guess some secrets are best left buried."

Asia traced her finger through the dust on one of the windowsills. "I liked Mary Wintergreen. I still think of her as Mary Wintergreen, even though I know she was really Miranda's ghost. She seemed real, not like a ghost at all."

"I have a theory about this," said Beth. "At Cold Creek, Miranda's ghost was tormented by her memories. She wanted so desperately to make contact with you, but her pain and fear hindered her."

"She tried," said Asia. "That last night on the bridge, I think she was coming to see me, and then she lost her nerve."

"And after that I whisked you away to West Vancouver," said Beth. "How amazing that you found her again."

"Or she found me," said Asia, thinking of the day when Monty stole her Saint Christopher medal.

"When Miranda was an old woman, she was probably at peace," said Beth. "As the years went by, she must have realized that no one would ever find out what she had done. So it was much easier for her to appear to you in the cottage. I think she made up the name Mary Wintergreen so you wouldn't be frightened away."

"At the end, I could hear her voice but I couldn't see her," said Asia. "That's when I knew she was a ghost. She must have started to disappear as soon as I found her diary."

"Because she knew it was almost over," said Beth. She sounded excited. She's probably thinking about her book, thought Asia. She peered up the sagging staircase. "Before we go, I want to have one more look at Daisy's bedroom."

Beth hesitated. "If those stairs held you once, they'll hold you again. I'll wait down here. But for heaven's sake, be careful."

Asia crept cautiously up the worn staircase and opened the door to Daisy's room. The room was bare, the old wooden floorboards covered in a layer of dirt and dust. The little pink bed and the dresser and the rocking chair were gone. She walked over to the window and touched a ragged strip of pink material nailed to the frame that she hadn't noticed before. A small blue button lay on the middle of the sill. Asia picked it up. Her heart gave a little thud. Was it a button off Miranda's long blue dress?

"Find something blue, your wish will come true," she whispered. She slipped it into her pocket and then leaned over the sill and looked at the little hill beside the creek. Beatrice had said that Daisy's grave was there, but she could see nothing except tall golden grass.

"The room's empty," she told Beth when she came back downstairs. "But I know I didn't dream the furniture."

"I think the furniture was real," said Beth, "just like all the furniture and things at Cormorant Cottage."

"Sierra saw everything at Cormorant Cottage," said Asia slowly. "And she heard Mary Wintergreen talk. So it's not just me. It's Sierra too."

"I know," said Beth, smiling. "It was one of the first things I thought of when you told me the story."

"It's just like you said," said Asia. "Talking to ghosts runs in our family."

"And right now you and Sierra are the lucky ones."

"Are we going to tell Sierra that Mary Wintergreen was a ghost?" said Asia.

"Do you think we should?"

Asia nodded vigorously. "No more secrets. Besides, she'll love it!"

Beth and Asia walked outside. The sky had deepened to navy blue, and the mountains glowed pale pink. There was a sharp cold bite in the air. "I just want to do one more thing before we go back," said Asia. "I want to see if I can find Daisy's grave."

Asia and Beth walked behind the house to the bank above the creek. Asia gazed around. The faded seed heads of a few scraggly thistles poked above the grass. "It must have been right here. But everything's so overgrown. I don't see anything."

"I expect it disappeared a long time ago." An icy wind blew up from the creek, and Beth shivered and dug her hands into her jacket pockets. "I'm ready to go back for some hot chocolate."

"Me too," said Asia.

Beth started walking briskly, and Asia took one last look around. She caught a glimpse of purple deep in the grass. She reached down and picked up a small bouquet of faded purple asters. "How did this get here?" she murmured. She looked at them for a minute and then gently laid them back on the ground. Her heart felt lighter as she ran to catch up to Beth.

~

Asia rested her back against the trunk of her climbing tree and gazed down at Cold Creek. A hint of fall was in the crisp air and in the touch of yellow on the aspen leaves. She and Beth were leaving tomorrow, and Maddy and Harry the day after. Cold Creek would be closed up for the winter.

But it will still be here, Asia thought. It will always be here. She took a deep breath and gazed at the meadows and the mountains and the creek. If only there were some way to put a piece of everything in her wolf box and bring it out when she needed it. Two deer bounded across the meadow on the other side of the creek. For a second, she imagined she saw Ira striding toward the bridge in his familiar plaid jacket, his arms swinging. Tears pressed against the back of her eyes. "We're coming back," she whispered. "Migrating birds always come back."

Voices from the garden drifted up to her. Beth and Maddy were picking the last of the cabbages and turnips, and Harry was gathering up stray shovels and hoes. Asia slipped her hand into her pocket and took out the little blue button. *Find something blue, your wish will come true.* She hadn't made her wish yet. There were so many things she could wish for, but right now she was fine. She would put the button in her box with her four-leaf clover, her special stone and Miranda's diary, and save it for when she really needed it. She slipped the button back into her pocket. She waited a few more minutes until she was ready and then scrambled down through the branches of the huge pine tree to join her family.

Becky Citra works as a primary school teacher and lives on a ranch in Bridge Lake, British Columbia. She is the author of numerous books for young readers, including the popular Max and Ellie historical series (Orca). When not teaching or writing, Becky cross-country skis, rides one of her five horses, watches the wildlife that visits her home and reads.

Acknowledgments

I would like to thank the British Columbia Arts Council for their support for this project. Thank you also to my sister Janet, who spent many many hours mulling over the initial drafts, to my mother, who is always ready to listen, and to my friend Helen for her excellent suggestions. I would like to thank my editor, Sarah Harvey, who did such a wonderful job of clarifying the difficult parts and defining the shape of the story.